the EMPTY DRAGON

STEVE DIXON

Other books in the *Rumours of the King* trilogy:

Out of the Shadows
What the Sword Said

Copyright © Steve Dixon 2004
First published 2004
ISBN 1 85999 746 5

Scripture Union, 207–209 Queensway, Bletchley, Milton Keynes, MK2 2EB, England.

Email: info@scriptureunion.org.uk
Website: www.scriptureunion.org.uk

Scripture Union Australia
Locked Bag 2, Central Coast Business Centre, NSW 2252
Website: www.su.org.au

Scripture Union USA
PO Box 987, Valley Forge, PA 19482
www.scriptureunion.org

British Library Cataloguing-in-Publication Data.

A catalogue record of this book is available from the British Library.

Printed and bound in Great Britain by Creative Print and Design (Wales) Ebbw Vale.

Cover: Hurlock Design

Scripture Union is an international Christian charity working with churches in more than 130 countries, providing resources to bring the good news about Jesus Christ to children, young people and families and to encourage them to develop spiritually through the Bible and prayer.

As well as our network of volunteers, staff and associates who run holidays, church-based events and school Christian groups, we produce a wide range of publications and support those who use our resources through training programmes.

FOR MY WIFE JANE
the leader of our gang

tbe STORY SO FAR

he land known as the Old Kingdom has been infested with dragons for longer than anyone can remember. The region around the town of Kiriath is plagued by one of these monsters. Through its servant, a man everyone simply calls 'The Reaper', this dragon sends constant demands for sacrifices from all the surrounding villages – crops, livestock, and sometimes even humans. When his sister Safir is chosen as a sacrifice, the twelve-year-old Ruel decides to act. He sets off on a quest to find help in rescuing Safir and ridding the area of its dragon. He plans to appeal to the King, but he has a problem – no one has seen or heard of any king in the Old Kingdom for more than a generation. Most inhabitants of the Kingdom doubt that a king even exists any more and no one knows where he might be found if he does.

While wandering in the forest that surrounds his village, Ruel meets a mysterious woodsman by the name of Baladan. He seems poor but he rides a magnificent warhorse called Hesed and carries a mighty sword. Later Baladan turns up at Hazar, Ruel's village, and offers to kill The Dragon if the villagers will help him. Only Ruel and his best friend, an old woman called Zilla, go with Baladan. The rest of the villagers hide away. Ruel's father, Maaz, thinks Baladan has abducted his son and leads a hunt for the woodsman, a hunt that ends in failure at the foot of the mountain where The Dragon lives.

During the hunt, a group of seven young men from Hazar unexpectedly find themselves joining Baladan – a hothead called Zethar, with his friend Chilion, and a group of five more friends led by a young man called Thassi. As Baladan journeys through the forest, he releases two sisters, Lexa and Rizpa, from the custody of The Reaper. They join his group, as does The Reaper himself – he turns out to be an old man called Zabad who has been an unwilling slave to The Dragon for many years. With these additions, Baladan now has a group of twelve followers and he leads them against The Dragon, finally destroying it and rescuing Safir before disappearing as mysteriously as he came.

Baladan leaves word, however, that there is more work to do and that the twelve friends must wait for instructions. They wait from summer to winter before receiving a message that they are to meet Baladan at a remote castle by the sea at the far western end of the Old Kingdom. The twelve make the hazardous journey and arrive at the castle, which belongs to Earl Rakath, just in time for the New Year festivities. During the feast a messenger arrives from Earl Melech, the most powerful of the four Earls of the Old Kingdom, announcing a Great Tournament to be held in the autumn. News of Baladan's victory over The Dragon of Kiriath has spread, and with it, the hope that the dragons could actually be defeated and the Kingdom cleansed of them. The purpose of Earl Melech's tournament is to find a Champion who will then be given command of a Grand Army to lead against the dragons.

As they wait for their rendezvous with Baladan at Rakath's castle, the twelve friends equip themselves with weapons and learn how to use them, assuming that they and Baladan will be entering the Tournament so that Baladan can become Champion. However, when Baladan finally arrives, he tells the friends they must leave their weapons behind and set off in small groups on a series of strange missions. Everywhere they go during their travels, the friends hear tales of Abaddon. He is a fearsome robber chief who controls the centre of the Kingdom, and he is going to enter the Tournament. He has sent his men all over the land, threatening and bribing people to support him in the coming contest.

The friends and Baladan are finally reunited with each other at a tiny derelict castle on the western border. Only Zethar is missing – he has been sent off on his own on a mysterious quest. At the castle they meet Jalam, the son of the castle's owner. He is desperate to take part in the Tournament and Baladan has made him armour and weapons. The friends travel to Earl Melech's lands in the east of the Kingdom, and the forces gather for the Tournament but Baladan refuses to take part or allow the twelve to join in the contest. They are disappointed and confused, but Zethar is beside himself. He has returned from his mission with news of having encountered a Great Dragon. It has terrified him and he is desperate for someone to lead an army to destroy it. Baladan says he will meet the Great Dragon but without an army. This seems like madness to Zethar and he has a secret meeting with Abaddon in which he agrees to help the robber if he will lead an army against the Great Dragon.

Abaddon's force on the day of the Tournament includes some people the friends have met on their travels: Oreb, a bandit from the northern border lands; Zemira, a young lord from the southern coast who is a minstrel and studies chivalry; and Shamma, an old man who has a fantasy that he is a knight. Also in Abaddon's ranks is Halak, the blacksmith from Ruel's village – he, like many, has been persuaded that the only hope for the Kingdom is in Abaddon's strength. The forces opposing Abaddon include Sir Achbor, a knight whom Baladan had befriended in Kiriath, and Jalam. Jalam eventually wins the contest, defeating Abaddon in single combat, but the robber kills him and Abaddon's thugs intimidate Earl Melech into awarding their chief the Champion's crown.

CHAPTER ONE

She just walked out of the flames. Amm and Peth stopped in their tracks and gawped at the impossible. A girl of about fourteen, dressed in smoking rags, had walked out of a blazing building right in front of them. It was burning so fiercely inside that they wouldn't even have considered trying to tackle the fire or look for survivors. Then, as they watched dumbfounded, the whole interior of the house caved in on itself with a thunderous rumble and a crash, sending a blast of flame, hot air and debris out of the doorway. The girl was blown towards them and the two men were jerked out of their stupor, launching themselves forward to catch her. She stared at them as they supported her, recognising by their dark green jackets that they were members of the Mesaloth city garrison.

'They're dead,' she murmured, then collapsed, unconscious.

There was no time to hang around. This wasn't the only building alight – the whole neighbourhood was burning and fire was still raining down from the grey, February sky. As Amm hoisted the girl onto his shoulders there was a whooshing that could be heard even above the roaring flames then a great thump as another fireball landed in a blazing explosion on a house further up the narrow street.

'Run!' Amm shouted to his companion and the pair of them set off at full speed.

They were heading for their barracks where they'd been ordered to take any injured citizens they managed to rescue from the burning streets of Mesaloth.

On the way, they passed many more of the city's

garrison, struggling to douse fires, pull survivors from wrecked buildings, or herd people to places of safety – out of range of the huge catapults that were launching the flaming missiles at Mesaloth. The city was the largest in the Old Kingdom and the space inside its walls was packed with houses, shops and the premises of various manufacturers. Almost everywhere a fireball fell, it set light to one of these buildings and at once, the place would erupt into frantic activity: screaming occupants, fighting their way out onto the streets, sometimes on fire themselves; soldiers of the garrison rushing up with buckets of water to do what they could to quench the flames; a bucket chain quickly set up to the nearest of the city's many wells; the squad officer bellowing orders at his men; collapsing roofs and walls; and dead bodies carried out amidst the shrieks of their families. The bombardment of the city had started at noon, and the garrison had been ordered out straight away. Amm, Peth and the rest of them had now been at work in this blazing nightmare for two hours and they were exhausted.

The garrison barracks consisted of a set of dormitory blocks built against the defensive wall of the city. They were sheltered from the almost constant rain of fireballs and other missiles that had been launched into Mesaloth during the eight weeks it had been under siege, and because of this, some of the blocks had been turned into first aid posts. It was to one of these that Amm and Peth took their latest patient, unloading her onto one of the rough wooden beds that had been knocked together for the injured. There were dozens of other beds crammed in the low, dark room, each with at least one person lying on it, moaning and groaning. There was no one to look after them – that would have to wait. The guards who brought them in just dumped them and ran back to their duties. Peth was about to do likewise when Amm stopped him.

'Hang on!' he shouted, above the noise in the room.

'What?' Peth answered.

'I don't think this one's really injured. I can't see any blood. Can you see anything?'

Peth gave her a quick glance.

'So?' he asked.

'So she shouldn't be taking up a bed. Maybe if we can bring her round…'

'We can send her packing.'

'Not what I had in mind,' Amm answered. 'I was thinking that maybe we could take her to our block, give her something to eat, find out who she belongs to.'

'And by the time we've done all that, the attack'll be over,' shouted Peth, impatiently.

'Exactly,' Amm replied, passing a hand over his sweating forehead. He was worn out and determined to take a break.

Peth was a teenager, hardly older than the girl they were standing over, and Amm was in his forties – old enough to be Peth's father. There was no question about who would get their own way.

Minutes later, they were out of the din of the first aid station and Amm had their patient propped up in a chair in the little guard room at the end of the block where he and Peth were billeted. The girl was awake and although she didn't seem to have strength to move any other part of her body, her eyes were moving restlessly, taking in every detail of her surroundings.

'What's your name?' Amm asked.

She fixed him for a moment with those eyes – hard and slate grey – then erupted into a fit of racking coughs. She struggled for some time to get control of her smoke-scoured lungs before she could answer.

'Nara,' she said, at last – and she snapped the word out, as if she was daring him to have anything to say about it.

'What's yours?'

'I'm Amm,' he told her, rather taken aback, 'and this is Peth. We're going to give you something to eat, then we'll take you to find your family.'

Nara glared. 'That'll be hard,' she said. 'They're all dead.'

Amm felt stupid, considering the circumstances in which they'd found her.

'I'm sorry,' he said, gently. 'I suppose they were in the house.'

He thought of his own wife and children, in the little cottage they rented in one of the poorer quarters of Mesaloth, and hoped desperately that they were safe just now.

Nara didn't respond to the softness of his tone. She went on staring at him in a way that made him look at the stone-flagged floor.

'They died weeks ago,' she snapped. 'It was my children in the house.'

'Your brothers and sisters?'

'Just children,' she replied. 'War orphans like me. I found them wandering in the ruins. I was looking after them. The house seemed a good place to stay. Must have been hit weeks ago – abandoned, but not much damage. Perfect hideout. Then the roof fell in when the fireball hit it today – killed them all – set the place blazing.'

Amm felt a weight of sadness inside him. The siege of Mesaloth had been going on so long that there were droves of orphans like Nara, roaming the city in little gangs, fending for themselves as best they could amongst the wrecked and deserted houses. And it wasn't just the enemy – Abaddon's besieging army – that was killing people now: starvation and disease were starting to make orphans of the city's children as well as fire and steel.

'What happened to your family, then?' Amm asked, determined not to be put off by the harshness of her replies.

Nara struggled to straighten herself in her chair, and a look of fierce pride came into her face.

'My father was killed in the first attack,' she told him. 'He was a knight of the castle.'

Amm asked her father's name, and he recognised it. When Abaddon's army had first marched on Mesaloth, just before the New Year, the city governor, Baron Medan, had led his castle knights and their men out to do battle. From all accounts, Nara's father had fought bravely at the head of a squadron of cavalry, but in the end he had died with hundreds of others as Abaddon's troops had crushed the men of Mesaloth and driven them back behind their city walls – where they had stayed for the past two months. Amm looked at the state Nara was in. Her father had been a rich man, and here was his daughter in rags, her nails cracked and dirty, face filthy with smoke, living like an animal. Amm felt very tired. He leaned against the bare stone wall of the guard room and wondered what hope there was left for the city.

'What happened to the rest of your family?' he asked her.

'House caught fire,' she said, dully. 'Burned alive – mother, brother, two sisters, six servants.'

'And you?'

'I don't seem to be meant to burn,' she said. 'Today's the third fire I've got out of.'

Nara's head with its matted ginger curls drooped a little but her voice lost none of its sharpness.

'I just wish I could get *other people* out,' she said. 'I promised those children I'd take *care* of them.'

'And so you did, I'm sure,' Amm told her, 'as best you could. I shouldn't think anyone could have done any better. Now it's time for someone to look after *you* for a change. Be our guest – we've only got a scrape or two of oats, but you're welcome to share them.'

At this, a look of desperation came over Peth's face. The winter food stocks were running out and the whole city was on rations. It was madness to say they'd feed this Nara – they had nothing spare to give her.

'*Isn't* she, Peth?' Amm said, sternly. 'Go and fetch the pot for our visitor.'

'No need,' said Nara. 'You can have some of what *I've* got.'

Her ragged clothes were the kind a servant boy would wear, and she started rummaging inside her thick canvas jerkin.

'Here!' she said, and held out a scrawny brown rat, dangling it by its tail.

Peth looked as if he was going to retch but Amm took hold of the creature and started looking it over to see how fresh it was.

'Not bad,' he said. 'Where did you get it?'

'I'm good at catching them,' she said. 'I'll get you some more if you want.'

'No, *thank* you,' Peth said, in disgust.

'Get used to it,' Amm told him. 'We'll all be eating them soon.'

There was a thump and a roar as another fireball landed nearby.

'If we last that long,' Amm added, and went off to cook the rat.

❦

When it came to it, Peth ate his share without any fuss, and he wouldn't have refused an extra helping if there'd been one. But he seemed to be brooding about something.

'What did you mean, "If we last that long"?' he asked, after a while.

'Haven't you noticed anything?' Amm said, waving towards the window. The sights and sounds and stink of the inferno were as strong as ever and fireballs were still falling. 'This is the longest bombardment they've ever thrown at us. Don't you think it means something?' Amm went on.

'They're going to storm the walls,' Nara said, quietly.

'There you are – she's got more sense than you have,' Amm told the youngster.

'But we'll push them back,' Peth said, stoutly.

Amm shook his head. 'I wish I had your confidence,' he said.

'But we've *got* to,' the young man insisted. 'Mesaloth's the most powerful city in the whole of the Kingdom – we *can't* let Abaddon take it. We're all that's holding Abaddon's army up. If *we* go, the road's clear for his forces to march straight on to Earl Jamin's fortress. And if *that* goes, the war's as good as lost. We've *got* to hold out – for Baladan's sake.'

Amm made a spitting sound. 'Don't say that name to me,' he replied. 'If you ask me, that man's been nothing but trouble. I don't know *why* this city's supporting him. It's all right Baron Medan having a council of his knights to decide what to do, but did anyone ever ask the *people* of Mesaloth what they wanted? Not likely. Because if they had, I'll tell you what reply they'd have got: "Abaddon's army's coming, so let's put up Abaddon's flag on all our towers then they'll go on their way and leave us in peace.".'

'That's not what *I'd* have said,' Peth told him.

'Well you're a fool,' Amm replied, slapping his knee impatiently. 'And so's Baron Medan – which surprises me, because he's old enough to know better.' Then he sighed and smiled at his young companion. Peth was a neighbour's boy, and Amm had promised to take care of him for her.

'But that's more than can be said for you,' he conceded. 'So I suppose I ought to make allowances.'

Peth went red in the face. 'Look,' he said, '*Baladan* should be leading the Grand Army, not Abaddon. Baladan's proved what he can do. He's killed The Dragon of Kiriath, and he's the one to lead the Old Kingdom against the power of the dragons. It's *him* that can set us free, not Abaddon. Who *is* Abaddon, anyway? Just some jumped-up robber, that's all – what right has he to claim he can lead the Army of the Old Kingdom?'

'You *know* what right he has,' Amm told him, wearily. '*Everyone* knows. Earl Melech held his Tournament last autumn to *decide* who should lead the Grand Army against the dragons, and Abaddon *won* – fair and square. Baladan didn't even turn up. Why we have to have a civil war about it, I can't understand.'

There was a moment's silence, then Nara spoke.

'Actually, it wasn't fair and square,' she said.

They both looked at her in surprise.

'How do *you* know?' Amm asked, a little put out. 'Were you there?'

'No,' she said, 'but my father was. He said someone called Jalam won it and that he was fighting *on behalf* of Baladan. But then Abaddon came up behind him after the fighting was supposed to be over and killed him. Abaddon cheated.'

'What does it matter?' Amm asked. 'Jalam's dead and Baladan's disappeared – if he ever existed in the first place. That's what's so ridiculous – I can't for the life of me work out why half the Kingdom has decided to support someone who can't even be *found*. Why have this civil war when there's only one man left to claim the throne?'

'What do you mean, "Claim the throne"?' Peth asked. 'Who said anything about that? The Tournament was supposed to be about who leads the Grand Army – that's what this *war's* about. It's nothing to do with being King.'

Amm shook his head with a sad smile. 'I do wish you'd grow up,' he said. 'When he's beaten everyone who stands in his way – which he will – do you think Abaddon's really going to be satisfied with anything less than the crown? And good luck to him, I say. Once he's crowned King, that'll be that. He can't be uncrowned, and nobody will fight against the King. Perhaps there'll be a bit of peace at last – and if we're *very* lucky, we might still be alive to enjoy it.'

'But he *can't* be crowned King,' Peth protested. 'There still *is* a king.'

'Maybe,' Amm pointed out.

'All right – maybe,' the young man admitted. 'But nobody's proved there *isn't* one.'

'And nobody's seen any *sign* of a king in this land for more than a generation. If there *is* one, he must be like this Baladan we're all risking our lives for – *invisible*. I'd rather put my trust in someone I can see.'

Peth was getting more and more upset. 'But Abaddon's a cheat,' he said. 'Her father said so. He might be the only one we can see but how can anyone trust a cheat? I'd rather fight for Baladan's *name* even if I can't see him – even if *no one's* seen him – I'd rather fight just for his *name* than for a dozen Abaddons, no matter how real they are.'

Amm stood up and turned his back on Peth as if there was no point in continuing the discussion.

'Now you're just being stupid,' he said, and he went to look out of the window at his burning city.

'*You* support Baladan, don't you?' Peth turned to Nara.

Nara was kicking her heels against the floor, seeming completely uninterested.

'You can't support *Abaddon!*' Peth went on. 'Not after what your father told you.'

Nara looked up and fixed Peth with her hard grey eyes.

'I support me,' she said. 'I'm all I've got left.'

At that moment, a sound cut through the commotion outside that proved Nara right about the plans of the besieging army. It was a series of trumpet blasts signalling all forces to defend the walls.

'This is it, then,' Amm said. 'Come on, Peth – now's your chance to fight for the invisible man.' He turned to Nara. 'You'd better stay here,' he told her as he and Peth picked up their weapons and headed for the door. Nara didn't reply. She watched from the window until her two guardians had disappeared into the tide of rushing soldiers, then she slipped out herself.

The barrack block was close to the city gates and Nara could see a good stretch of the wall when she got outside. Even though she'd expected it, what she saw sent a chill through her. The tops of scaling ladders were visible all along the wall and the men of the Mesaloth garrison had not been able to push them off. Abaddon's soldiers had a firm foothold and seemed to be taking control in several places. Even more frightening, ugly siege towers could be seen looming over the wall in key positions. Abaddon's men were raining arrows down from these towers onto the defending forces and driving them off the walkways. It was obvious to Nara what was happening: there just weren't enough of the garrison to put up a defence because so many of them were still trapped in the city streets where, like Amm and Peth, they'd been trying to deal with the results of the bombardment. It was also obvious to her what was *going* to happen: the walkways were going to be overrun, and very soon. Nara took to her heels and headed for the city centre – as far away from the wall as she could get.

But Nara couldn't move fast enough. Too many streets and alleyways were blocked by fire, smoking rubble or hysterical crowds.

She heard the shout go up: 'They're over the wall!'

And minutes later: 'There's fighting by the gates!'

Then: 'They're in the market place!' 'They've taken the east!' 'They're coming from the west!'

Hordes of people were surging, first this way then that, around the network of streets. There was no telling which direction – or directions – the danger was coming from and soon Nara was as confused as the masses of panicking people who now seemed to fill every thoroughfare. The citizens of Mesaloth were being bunched together like fish caught in a tightening net. And then Nara was in among the fighting herself. She turned a corner and saw, no more than fifty metres ahead of her, a squad of about twenty garrison men come rushing out of a side alley. An officer shouted orders and they hastily formed up across the street with a shield row at the front, then half a dozen pike men bracing their long weapons in place between the shields, and finally, a group of archers behind, ready to fire over their companions' heads.

No sooner were they in place than the far end of the street filled up with Abaddon's men, who came charging towards them. The archers cut down many of them but still they came on. More were skewered on the pikes but others just kept coming – unstoppable as the tide. They clambered over their own dead and dying, hungry to get to grips with the Mesaloth men, and it took only moments for the little defensive position to be overwhelmed. Swords swung and lunged, there was a crescendo of yells and clashing metal, then it was all over and Abaddon's men were rushing on down the street, leaving a pile of mangled bodies behind them. Nara turned and fled. She felt a swish of air past her face and heard an arrow clatter against the wall of a building just beside her. It was a house, its door ajar, so she threw herself inside, trusting that the soldiers behind her were too busy to follow. She was right – the detachment of Abaddon's men raced past and was gone.

The house was abandoned and Nara decided to climb onto the roof to see what was happening. She managed to break through the tiles in the attic without much difficulty and soon she was standing astride the roof ridge, hanging onto the chimney and surveying the burning wreck of her city. The first thing she looked for was activity on the walls, but there was none. Clearly the garrison had given them up and all fighting was now down in the streets of Mesaloth. These were so narrow that it was impossible for Nara to see into them, even from a roof top, but she guessed that the fierce fight she had just witnessed must be being repeated a hundred times over throughout the city. And she guessed that the result would be the same each time. One thing she *could* see from her roof was that the city gates were wide open and Abaddon's forces were marching through them in vast numbers. The city of Mesaloth was plainly lost.

Baron Medan's castle stood on a mound in the northern corner of the city and Nara knew that the remains of the garrison would be retreating to it. Abaddon's soldiers would obviously know this too, and she was sure they would be battling to cut off the garrison and citizens. Nara got her bearings then clambered back through the roof, took the house stairs two at a time, crashed out onto the street and made a dash for the castle.

It was a nightmare journey. Time and time again she skidded to a halt, finding the way ahead blocked by fighting as units of the garrison tried desperately to hold up the enemy advance; or she would come upon a whole street full of Abaddon's men, with nothing to stand against them, marching in good order towards the castle. Whichever way she turned, she seemed to find herself *behind* the line of Abaddon's advancing troops. And when she finally emerged from the streets onto Castle Green – the broad area of open ground in front of the castle gate – she realised she'd failed. The Green sloped up towards the castle and on this rising ground she saw that several ranks of Abaddon's soldiers had already been drawn up. Even more terrible was the fact that beyond Abaddon's men were about a hundred citizens and soldiers of Mesaloth who had been unable to get through the castle gate before the drawbridge had been raised. They were now trapped between the castle and the enemy, and Nara watched in horror as Abaddon's men gave a roaring cheer and charged, cutting them to pieces in no time.

Nara turned back to the burning city. She realised that her only hope now was to run *away* from the castle – to get *out* of Mesaloth altogether and make for the forest. Once more, she set off into the maze of streets, heading this time for the city gate. Her sharp wits kept her out of danger for five minutes but then she emerged from an alley and found herself face to face with a squad of Abaddon's men, their leather jerkins splashed with blood, swords dripping with it, clearly thirsty for more. They were ten strides ahead of her and she just had time to bolt back the way she'd come. But now that the battle for the city was won, the enemy had time to hunt down every last inhabitant: the men gave a shout and came straight after her. She was light on her feet and they were laden with weapons and tired from battle so she began to gain on them; but the buildings she was running between were smouldering wrecks and suddenly, with a rumble and a crash, the whole side of one of them collapsed ahead of her, turning her escape route into a dust-filled dead end. A bouncing piece of debris gouged her cheek and she swung round in a desperate search for a way out. She had a rubble barricade behind her, blank walls on either side, and a gang of savage men charging towards her, roaring like animals.

ChAPTER TWO

nce the city was won, Abaddon's soldiers began to organise themselves in Mesaloth. The division that had mounted the attack reformed in front of the castle to rest and celebrate the victory by gloating over the trapped remnant of the garrison. Meanwhile, a division of fresh troops moved into the city and split into three brigades, each of which combed methodically through a different area. Their job was to mop up. That meant stripping each building of its valuables and butchering any survivors they could find. The troops positioned in front of the castle might have been angry that soldiers who hadn't fought to conquer the streets were taking all the plunder but they knew that these men would not be keeping the goods for themselves. Everything stolen from any city or village had to be sent straight back to the robber chief himself at his headquarters in the centre of the Kingdom. Torture and death were in store for anyone who broke this rule, and no one did. Abaddon made sure his soldiers were well paid and they didn't complain.

The general was the best paid of all the soldiers in this army that Abaddon had sent to conquer the south of the Old Kingdom. As evening turned to night, trumpets blared, the besieging troops came to attention in endless battalions around the castle and Abaddon's general rode out towards the castle gate, with his officers in a group behind him. The trumpets continued to sound and the general waited within shouting distance of the walls until the castle garrison had all turned out and the knights of Mesaloth with their leader, Baron Medan, were gathered on top of the gatehouse. The Baron had ordered everyone to carry a torch up onto the castle battlements to make a brave show of defiance but their lights looked puny compared to the sight that met them below. The general had had the same idea and the torches held by his troops made Castle Green look like a carpet of fire. Even more depressing for the garrison was the sight they could see dimly behind the besieging forces, lit by flickering torchlight and the moon. It was the dark outline of shattered buildings, from many of which the smoke still drifted – the wreck of their city, now crawling with enemy troops.

The general was a small man and he sat on a small horse – more like a pony than a knight's warhorse – but both horse and rider seemed to be charged with energy, shifting impatiently as if waiting was not in their nature. The general wore only a breastplate and his head was bare. When he judged the moment was right, he glared up at the company high above him on the gatehouse as if daring anyone to fire down at him.

'I'm Oreb,' he bellowed, 'general of Earl Abaddon's army in the south. And in the Earl's name, I call upon you to surrender.'

'What name?' Baron Medan shouted back. 'A stolen one! But then your master always was a thief. He's no more an earl than I am!'

'He was given his title by Melech, greatest Earl of the Kingdom, at the New Year feast,' Oreb replied.

'It needs all *four* Great Earls to give a title,' Baron Medan protested. 'Even a child knows that.'

Oreb drew a short, mean-looking sword and raised the blade high in the air.

'This is what gives titles, my friend,' he shouted, 'and if you think any different, perhaps you'd like to come down here and prove your point with your own weapon.'

Oreb's voice had become sharper and its northern accent

more harsh. His words bounced off the castle walls and there was no reply.

'I thought as much,' Oreb mocked. 'Face it, Baron – your position's hopeless. I've got enough men down here to pull your castle to pieces and take a stone each for a trophy. Surrender and have done with it, man – why suffer any more?'

'Never!' Baron Medan bellowed. 'We will never surrender to a robber's mob, however many you are! If you want every stone of this castle, we'll make you *fight* for every stone!'

The Baron was an impressive looking man, thickset, with a broad chest, wild iron-grey hair and deep dark eyes. It wasn't cowardice that had stopped him taking up Oreb's challenge to single combat, but the certain knowledge that even if he'd won, Oreb's men would have cut him to pieces. Without their leader, the people of Mesaloth would have surrendered at once, and all would have been lost. The garrison knew this as well as Medan and they rallied to his defiance with a cheer.

'People of Mesaloth,' Oreb shouted, 'Earl Abaddon is your rightful leader – winner of the Great Tournament, ruler of all but a few rebellious corners of the Kingdom. Do you really want to die for a stubborn baron?'

'They won't die for me – they'll die for Baladan!' Medan roared back. 'When Abaddon was proclaimed Champion at the Tournament, it was not so that he could *rule* us but so that he could *lead* us against the dragons, and I hear no news of him doing that. My lands are plagued by a dragon like none other in the whole of the Kingdom. It has taken our crops and our people for generations and it could scorch your army to a cinder before your swords were even drawn. We'll open our gates for no one but the Champion who will rid us of our Great Dragon, and that Champion's name is Baladan! Soon he will be with us, and his army will scatter your rabble like rubbish in the wind.'

'What army?' Oreb taunted. 'He *has* no army! Just bands of fools like you.'

The exchange went no further. There was nowhere else for it to go. Both sides were determined. Both knew that unless Baron Medan was right about Baladan, the castle would fall. And both sides had a similar estimate about the likelihood of Baladan turning up in time. Medan set his guards and went to lie, sleepless and hungry, on his bed. Oreb gave orders for the billeting of troops and called his officers to his tent for a celebration. And in the dark streets of broken Mesaloth a heap of rubbish heaved as if it had come to life. After a moment, a head emerged and a pair of sharp grey eyes darted left and right. There was silence and stillness. Oreb's men had long since finished their slaughter and gone to their tents. Slowly, Nara pulled her body out of the stinking mound.

In the few seconds before the charging soldiers would have reached her, she'd spotted a narrow passage between two houses. She'd hurtled down it and found herself in an enclosed court. It had clearly been a stable yard. The horses had long since been killed for food but in the centre there was still a large pile of filthy straw from the mucking out, mixed with all the other rubbish of the household that couldn't possibly be eaten. She'd seen that it was big enough to hide her and with the soldiers only moments behind, she hadn't had time to think twice so she'd scrabbled into the middle of the soggy heap and waited. A couple of minutes later, she felt the straw stir and something cold and hard slid against her arm. She knew it was the flat of a sword blade that had been thrust into the mound. If the soldier tried again, thrusting his sword the slightest bit to the right, the point would go clean through her. But he didn't. Time passed and nothing more happened. Still, she decided to stay where she was until she felt sure that night had fallen.

Now, as Oreb's troops turned their minds to eating and sleeping, Nara crept to the entrance of the passageway and peered out onto the street where she'd nearly died. The heap of rubble still barred her way to the left but to the right, the street was clear. Her legs were cramped and stiff but she made herself move quickly, darting from one piece of cover to another – now an entrance, now a pile of debris and sometimes a heap of bodies. The clear-up would start tomorrow before rotting set in and disease began to spread but for now, the dead of both sides had been left where they'd fallen. It was as she was crouching behind one of these gruesome piles that Nara realised she would have to change her fouled clothes. The slimy centre of the muck heap had soaked them and the stench would attract attention at twenty metres. Her only hope was to take the clothes from one of the corpses heaped in front of her so she began to look for a body of about her own size. After a moment, she saw one lying face down, just beyond the main pile. He was a soldier of the garrison, and as she pulled at his dark green jacket he shifted so that his face came into view. It was Peth.

Nara was stunned, but only for a moment. Feeling sorry for people was a luxury she couldn't afford just now. She went back to her work and soon she was cursing Peth because she couldn't pull his jacket off. She tried to roll him on his back but he wouldn't move, then she realised he was somehow attached to the body below him. She saw that a splintered spear was skewered clean through the chest of the man underneath, out of his back, and into Peth. It had obviously killed them both. Looking Peth over, she could see he had a terrible wound that had laid open his right thigh, and from the way they were lying on each other, it looked as if the man beneath had been carrying Peth on his back when the pair of them had been speared. When she looked at the face of the man under Peth, she wasn't surprised to see that it was Amm.

The bodies were stiff but at last she managed to work Peth free of the steel point lodged in his chest and pull off his jacket and breeches. He really hadn't been much older than she was and his white body looked skinny and pathetic in the moonlight. Nara covered it with her own wet clothes and slipped away down the street. She realised that being dressed in a guard's uniform might be a danger and Peth's caked blood on the slashed leg of his breeches scraped her skin, but at least she was dry now.

She made for the gate, in the hope that victory had made Oreb's men careless about guarding their newly captured prize. But when she got to within spying distance, she could see that she was going to be disappointed. The gateway was barred and sentries were posted. Even worse, she could see from the lights in their windows that the barrack blocks where Amm and Peth had taken her had now been occupied by the conquerors so this area of the city was probably one of the most dangerous. She breathed deeply and steadily until her heart stopped thumping and she could think clearly, and almost at once she noticed something that made her smile.

Looming over the city wall, only about a hundred metres to the right of the gate, was the ugly square outline of one of the siege towers that had been used to storm the walls.

'I bet that's not guarded,' she said to herself, and carefully, she crept towards it. She would have to climb onto the walkway round the walls, of course, and that would mean using an exposed set of stone steps, but she would just have to take the risk. The moon was clouding over now and if she moved confidently, she might be taken for one of the invading soldiers, at a distance.

When it came to it, Nara wasn't challenged. She made it onto the walkway in no time and couldn't see anyone guarding the wooden bridge that had been lowered from the siege tower onto the battlements. In her best imitation of a sentry, she marched up to the bridge and over it onto the platform at the top of the tower. It had a wooden roof to keep off missiles and was deep in shadow. At her first step, her foot kicked something big and heavy and she realised it was a body. It wasn't the only one. Slowly, she picked her way to the centre of the platform where she guessed the ladder up the inside of the tower would be. Her probing foot found the top of it and she climbed carefully down in total darkness, her heart jumping at every creak and crack of the wood. At last Nara found herself standing in the doorway through which hundreds of soldiers had poured that day to capture what was left of her home. She took a step forward and felt grass beneath her feet. The conquerors were behind her, and five hundred metres in front lay the forest and freedom. The moon was completely clouded over now and all that could be seen of Nara was a tiny, flitting patch of dark against a greater darkness as she slipped away from her city and its dead.

A broad river, the biggest in the Old Kingdom, flowed beneath the northern wall of Mesaloth. The forest was south of the city and several streams flowed out of it to join this great river. Early in the morning after the city fell, Nara was crouching on the bank of one of these streams with her head completely under water. The water was so icy that it made her head ring but still she stayed under as long as she could, combing her fingers through her curly hair and rubbing her face. She came up gasping but straight away took a deep breath and plunged her head back in. Three times she did this before she finally struggled over the slippery stones at the edge of the stream and lay down panting on a carpet of moss beneath the trees. Nara looked at her hands. The fingers were white from loss of circulation but at least they were clean. She ran them through her hair. The foul crust that had dried in her curls from yesterday's adventure was gone at last and her hair squeaked. Resting on the soft moss, she might almost have felt content if it hadn't been for the hunger relentlessly twisting her stomach.

Nara had been good at catching rats in the city but that was because she was a city girl. Legend had it that somewhere in the depths of the forest was the haunt of the Great Dragon – the beast that terrorised the whole region – so city people didn't venture amongst the trees. Nara had no survival skills outside the walls of Mesaloth and she wondered how on earth she was going to live. She might come across nuts and mushrooms, she supposed, but one thing she *did* know about the forest was that many of the things you found there were poisonous. You had to know what was what to make sure you were safe, and she didn't. It seemed hopeless but it wasn't in Nara's nature to give up. She'd survived this far through fire and sword, and deep inside, she never doubted that she would continue to do so. She just had to keep going. So she hauled her aching body upright, rubbed her hands back to life on the rough sleeves of Peth's jacket and set off in the opposite direction to the flow of the stream. She may not have been brought up amongst the trees but she had the brains to work out the route that would take her away from the city and danger.

Two hours later, Nara's head was swimming with tiredness and lack of food. She had heard plenty of creatures rustling amongst the bushes and fallen leaves and plenty of birds squawking and exploding through the branches above her but how she was going to catch any of them, she hadn't a clue. It was just as she was squinting up for the hundredth time at an escaping bird, trying to work out from its behaviour how she might capture one, that something captured her. The forest floor simply gave way, her stomach was launched into her chest and she crumpled into a heap with her legs twisted under her. Pain shot through her body and she yelped then rolled around, moaning and clutching her right ankle. Nara was in such agony that she retched but nothing came up from her empty stomach except a mouthful of bitter juices. She spat and rested her forehead on the earth until the pain died down enough for her to work out what had happened.

First she checked herself over. Her ankle was twisted but it wasn't broken and neither was anything else. She stood up and found that she could walk but she knew she'd be limping for days. Not that that was a problem at the moment as she had nowhere far to walk – she was in the bottom of a pit. It was about three metres square, five metres deep, and obviously dug on purpose. She looked up and saw the broken covering of branches and fern fronds she'd tumbled through. She'd clearly fallen into someone's trap. So *that* was how you caught animals in the forest – big ones, anyway.

Well, she *wasn't* an animal so she wasn't going to wait around and be captured. As soon as she was able, she set about trying to climb the walls of the pit. Her throbbing ankle didn't help but the climb was possible. There were plenty of roots poking out to give hand- and foot-holds, so it wasn't long before she'd managed to haul herself over the edge. She lay on her back on the forest floor, panting for a while, then scooped up a double handful of leaves and threw them into the air.

'Yes!' she hissed, clenching her fists.

At that moment, a shadow passed over her face and the end of a sharpened stave was jammed against her chest. She found herself staring up at a boy of about sixteen, dressed in rags, with murder in his eyes.

'Who are you?' he demanded.

Nara twisted as if she meant to get up and the boy pressed the wooden point harder against her.

'Move again and I'll kill you,' he said.

'Then you'll never find out who I am,' she told him, coolly.

The boy hesitated a fraction of a second and took the pressure off the stave. That was all Nara needed. He was standing astride her legs and in one movement she hooked her good foot behind one of his ankles, grabbed the end of the stave with both hands and heaved herself upwards. The sudden thrust on the stave sent the boy backwards and Nara's hooked foot caught his leg so that he crashed down onto the ground. She was up and about to throw herself on him when arms of varying sizes grabbed her from every side and she was held fast. She saw that she was being pinioned by about a dozen children, boys and girls aged from as young as five up to their teens, all dressed as raggedly as the boy who'd attacked her.

The fallen leader got up quickly and stood a pace in front of Nara, glaring. Then he spat in her face.

'You're wearing a Mesaloth uniform,' he said. 'Are you for Baladan?'

Nara glared back and her eyes were every bit as fierce as the boy's.

'Why?' she said. 'Are you for Abaddon?' And she spat straight back at him.

A young girl, who was hanging onto Nara's arm, giggled and the boy took a few steps away, wiping his face.

'Shut up, Penina!' he barked. Then he turned back to Nara. 'We're for no one but ourselves,' he said.

'Me, too,' Nara told him. 'Now will you get this lot off me? I don't mean you any harm.'

'You broke our trap,' the boy snapped but he didn't move close to her again.

'You nearly broke my ankle,' Nara replied.

One of the other youngsters snorted and Nara got the distinct impression they weren't used to anyone answering their leader back like this.

The boy threw his stave down and raised his fists.

'Let her go,' he barked at his gang; then, to Nara, 'Let's fight!'

Her captors stood back in a ring, and Nara squared her shoulders defiantly but she didn't put up her fists.

'That's not fair,' she said, in a firm, steady voice. 'I can hardly stand and I'm starving. Give me something to eat and let me rest *then* I'll fight you if you want.'

'You've got a cheek,' the boy said. 'Thanks to you, *we're* going to be starving now – we were hoping to take a deer in that,' and he gestured to the ruined trap.

'Or even a boar,' one of the youngsters piped up.

'You don't look to be doing too badly to me,' Nara said. 'I bet you've got something hidden away somewhere.' Then she pushed up her loose jacket sleeve to show her scrawny arm. 'Take a look at that,' she went on. 'I've just escaped from Mesaloth – we're all like that in there. We've been starving for weeks.'

As they stared at her wasted flesh, she scanned them all slowly, sizing them up. In the midst of all the action, her mind had been running fast, trying to work out who this gang of children might be.

'You're all war orphans, aren't you?' she said at last, looking from face to face again, and their sad-eyed silence gave her her answer.

There was a rumble of distant thunder and heavy drops of rain started to drum on the canopy of leaves high above them.

'We shouldn't be fighting,' she told them, 'I'm an orphan, too.'

She held her hand out to their leader. 'Nara,' she said.

The two eyed each other for a moment as the sound of the falling rain increased.

'I'm Aia,' the boy told her. He turned without taking her hand. 'Bring her,' he ordered.

The rain began to roar down on the forest roof as they marched away.

chapter three

aladan's young friend Ruel wondered how there could possibly be so much rain in the sky. It had been pouring down since morning and it was now the middle of the day. Not that he and the rest of Baladan's companions were getting wet. They'd found a surprisingly good shelter. Surprising because its walls were solid and it still had a good roof, yet it was the most ancient place Ruel had ever seen. It was a fortress, but it was like nothing that Ruel and his friends had come across in all their travels through the Old Kingdom. And between them they had travelled into almost every part of the Kingdom with Baladan, or under his orders, during the last couple of years.

The fortress looked as if it had been built for giants. They had approached it along a road as straight as an arrow and they'd seen the huge square marked out by its walls from miles away. When they got closer, they saw that there was a tower at each corner and that the road they were travelling on entered the fortress through a massively protected gateway in the middle of one wall. The place was built on a hillside sloping up in front of them so the whole layout was visible and they could see a similar gateway with a road coming through it in the middle of each of the other walls: the four roads met in the middle of the fortress. When they reached it, they found the gateway on their side open, its massive doors long since rotted, and they tramped through into what amounted to a small town. There were side streets coming off the four main roads at right angles – everything was at right angles – and these side streets were lined with buildings, every one of them deserted.

It was from the biggest of these buildings, possibly some

sort of headquarters, that Ruel was looking out at the rain falling on the cobbled street outside. He could see the ruts worn into the cobbles over many years by passing carts, and he wondered how long it was since a cart had rumbled along those stones, who had driven the last cart to leave the fortress and who had owned the place. Their three-day march along the straight road had seemed to take them out of the time and the world they knew into a hidden, forgotten corner of the Old Kingdom, abandoned for a thousand years.

The last people they'd seen had been a group of peasants from a village slightly north of the great city of Mesaloth. That had been just before Baladan had taken them onto the ancient road that led to the fortress.

'Don't go south,' the leader of the villagers had told them, his eyes full of fear, 'Abaddon's sent an army. There's soldiers everywhere.'

'What are they doing?' Baladan had asked. And he'd listened intently as the man described how Abaddon's army had been besieging Mesaloth for two months.

'And they're getting ready to use siege engines,' the villager told them. 'We've watched them building them for weeks, and now they're finished. They must be going to storm the city any day. There's no hope for Mesaloth, unless Baladan's army arrives. I should head north – it sounds as if things are quieter there.'

And with that, the villagers had hurried on their way as fast as if Abaddon's men were on their heels.

Ruel turned from the falling rain to look at his friends, scattered round the big room they were sheltering in. He remembered the argument there had been after those villagers had left. Although it had been three days ago, the bad feeling it had left still seemed to be hanging over them. Thassi and his four friends were playing a dice game in a corner and were snapping at each other over whose turn it was and who'd won what. They were strong, active young men in their twenties and they hated this wandering journey that Baladan was leading them on. As soon as they'd heard about the siege of Mesaloth, all they'd wanted to do was go and help. But Baladan would have none of it. Since the civil war had broken out, he hadn't allowed his friends to take part at all, always leading them away from any fighting they heard about.

The other two young men, Zethar and Chilion, were looking out at the rain, as Ruel had been doing but from separate windows. They'd been friends since they were boys in Hazar, the village almost all the twelve were from. But they hadn't spoken to each other since the argument about Mesaloth.

'I agree with Baladan,' Chilion had said. 'We *can't* go to help. What good would we be? But there *is* something we could do.'

Everyone had asked what it was. Chilion had explained that the villager talking about Baladan's 'army' had brought to a head something he'd been thinking about for days.

'We all know there *isn't* an army,' he'd explained, 'but there must be hundreds of groups like us, wandering the Kingdom, who'd fight for Baladan. We ought to be trying to find them, join them up, *make* an army. That way we'd be some use to places like Mesaloth.'

It had sounded a good idea and everyone had turned to Baladan for his reaction. But their leader had stayed silent. It was Zethar who'd spoken against the idea.

'No,' he had said. 'There's only one thing we have to do – we have to get Baladan to the Great Dragon.'

Chilion had lost his temper, accusing Zethar of having a one-track mind. Yes, the Great Dragon was important, Chilion had told him, but Zethar hadn't been able to think about anything else since they'd left the Tournament. Everyone had agreed and Chilion was leading an all-out attack on his friend before Baladan had broken things up.

'Zethar's right,' he'd told them. 'The Great Dragon comes first and it's Zethar's job to lead me to it. This war has blinded you to what's *really* wrong with the Old Kingdom – what's been destroying it for longer than anyone can remember. Tyrants like Abaddon come and go but it's the *dragons* that keep on wasting this land – and the only way to finally defeat *them* is to destroy their root – the Great Dragon that Zethar has found.'

Zethar was the only one of them who had seen this Great Dragon, and Baladan had given Zethar the job of taking him to its lair. But Zethar had not found it an easy task. They'd been travelling south since the Tournament but a journey that should have been over well before last winter had now taken them into the new year because Baladan had kept insisting they stop while he left them and went off on his own. He never told them where he was going or what he was doing but he was often away for days at a time. He was away now – he'd left them as soon as they'd reached this strange fortress that morning – and Ruel wondered who would break up the fight if Chilion and Zethar had a go at each other again.

Maybe the two young women who were with them could do it – the sisters Lexa and Rizpa from the village of Maon. They were the only two of Baladan's twelve who didn't come from Hazar and sometimes, being outsiders, they could smooth things over when tempers flared. There'd been many arguments since the Tournament. Usually they started because Baladan insisted on having no one with him but the twelve and they couldn't work out how he was going to take on the biggest dragon of all time without an army. Baladan would never explain and many times, when he was away, someone would ask why on earth they were still following this strange leader. A heated argument would follow. Zethar was always for going on, Chilion for deserting, and the others swung from one side to the other, depending on their mood. Invariably things would end with Lexa pointing out that Baladan *had* killed dragons before and should be trusted, or Rizpa telling them that they'd come this far together and they ought to stick together to the end.

Ruel was watching the sisters now. The room they were sheltering in was as big as a baron's hall and the two of them had been wandering round it for some time, pointing and whispering to each other. There were paintings all over the walls, huge figures in light flowing robes that looked as if they were designed for a warmer country than the Old Kingdom – but it was the floor the sisters were looking at. They came to a halt by a door on the opposite side of the room to the street and after a while, Rizpa looked up and caught Ruel's eye.

'Come and look at this,' she called to him.

At fourteen, Ruel was the youngest of the group, and the two sisters – Rizpa especially – had taken to mothering him. He usually found this annoying but just then, with the rain sheeting down, Baladan gone again and a storm brewing *inside* their shelter, Ruel felt glad to be treated like someone who needed his mind occupying.

When he joined the sisters, he saw straight away what was interesting them: the floor was made up of thousands of tiny coloured cubes that formed patterns – they'd all spotted that much when they'd arrived – but looking at the floor from where the sisters were, Ruel could see that there was more to it than that. They'd all been too bad tempered and preoccupied to notice anything else but now Ruel could see what the sisters had worked out – dulled by centuries of dust, there were pictures interwoven with the patterns on the floor, pictures which seemed to tell a story. Not only that, a major character in the story was a very fearsome-looking dragon.

There were two older members of the twelve – Zabad, who was in his fifties and had been a slave to The Dragon of Kiriath before Baladan freed him; and Zilla, who was in her seventies. The pair of them had been getting a fire going, but now Zilla came to see what Ruel and the sisters were looking at. She stared at the pictures in the floor, long and hard.

'Well, who'd have thought it?' she said, at last.

'What?' Ruel asked.

'I'd no idea the story was so old,' she went on.

'What story?'

'Why, the story of the first dragon, dearie,' she told him. 'Those pictures are telling the story of the first dragon there ever was. Fancy finding it here!'

Zabad had joined her and the dice players stood up to get a better look at the floor. Even Zethar and Chilion turned from their separate windows to see.

Zilla was a wonderful storyteller. People thought she was strange and she'd been something of an outcast in Hazar, but Ruel had spent a lot of time with her as he'd grown up and she'd often amazed him with her tales.

'Do you *know* the story?' Ruel asked her.

'Have I never told it to you, dearie?' she replied.

'I don't think so,' he said. 'Will you tell it now?'

The rain was still hissing down outside, splashing back ankle high from the ancient cobbled street. The fire was crackling and a pleasant warmth was starting to spread from it. Everyone was bored and fed up. There couldn't have been a better time for telling stories and Ruel's old friend didn't take much persuading.

'Once upon a time, a long time ago,' Zilla began, 'the whole world was a place of peace. There was no such thing as war, or even falling out. Everyone shared everything and there was always enough, because the earth made plenty of food on its own without digging and ploughing or sowing and reaping. The air smelled like perfume, the sun was always warm and everyone was happy. Young men and women married the people they loved, or loved the people they married, and their children were always strong, healthy and well behaved. No one was rich but then again, no one was poor. Everyone lived simply and well – better than we do now, for certain. Maybe it was something like that,' she said, and she pointed at the paintings on the walls.

She gave them a moment to look at the pictures. There were cracks and the plaster had fallen in places but the colours were still incredibly bright, even after centuries. The paintings showed tall, confident people in simple clothes walking in a landscape full of flowers. They looked very happy and beautiful.

'But then, one day,' Zilla went on, 'a man was out walking – just admiring the wonders of the world – when he saw something glinting beneath the shiny green leaves of a large bush. He was curious so he went to look and when he got close, he saw that the glinting was coming from an egg – a golden egg – cradled in a nest of leaves hidden beneath the bush. He reached into the shadows and picked up the egg. It was heavy and smooth and it felt good in his hand – it just fitted his palm. He held it up to the sun and it did more than shine – it shimmered in such a strange way that he could hardly take his eyes off it. Normally, he would have run excitedly back to his village to show everyone a wonderful find like this but something stopped him and after looking at it for a long time, he hid the egg inside his shirt. When he got back to his village, his neighbours called out 'hello' as they always did, but he ignored them and when he reached his home, he refused his food and snapped at his wife. All he wanted was to get into the bedroom and close the door so that he could gaze at his egg in private.

'He didn't come out of the bedroom for hours and his wife thought he was ill – something that rarely happened to anyone in those days until it was their time to die. That night, and every night that followed, the man slept with the egg nestled beside him in the secret shadows of the bed. He wrapped himself round it and turned his back on his wife. And during the days, he would carry the egg carefully inside his shirt, next to his warm skin. Everyone noticed the change in him – he became bad tempered and rude and sometimes spent all day in the bedroom. He invented a lock – something no one had ever thought of before – and put it on the bedroom door. Other times, he would go far away from the village where no one would follow him and he would spend hours on end gazing at his egg.

'For a month, the man hardly ate. He became thinner and thinner. All the village was at its wits' end. No one knew what to do because nothing like this had ever happened. And if anyone asked the man what was the matter, he'd threaten to hit them and say horrible things that people had never even *thought* before, let alone said. Then one morning, the village was woken by a terrible scream coming from the man's house. Everyone ran to see what was the matter. They found the wife in the bedroom with her hands over her face, howling and crying in a way no human being had ever been known to do. There was an empty eggshell on the bed, the floor was scorched and covered in blood, and there was a large hole in the back wall of the cottage.

'When she was able to speak, which wasn't for a long, long time, she told them what had happened. That morning, she'd been woken by strange noises that seemed to be coming from inside her bed – sounds like cracking and tearing. Then her husband had cried out in alarm. He'd squirmed towards her in the bed and the covers had fallen to one side. There, next to her husband, she'd seen the golden egg – and it was hatching. Both of them jumped out of the bed as a terrible screech came from the egg and it started to roll around. The man wept as the beautiful golden surface of his egg began to lose its shine and the cracks spread across it until it looked like baked mud.

"I held it too close," he blubbered, "I shouldn't have kept it so close. The heat has hatched it."

She'd put her arm round him and he had told her the whole story.

'They'd clung to each other and stared as the top was finally pushed off the egg and a small, green, scaly creature struggled out. It had leathery wings and smoke trailing from its nostrils and its eyes shone like gold. As they watched, it began to swell and grow. The wife backed away to the wall but her husband seemed rooted to the spot. When the thing was the size of a rabbit, it yawned, sending a spurt of fire across the room, and when it was the size of a wolf, it leapt at her husband and tore him to pieces, eating every bit. Then it simply crashed through the back wall, flapped its wings and took off into the dawn.

'No one knows where that egg came from,' Zilla concluded. 'Maybe it was there from the beginning of the world. But out of that first dragon has come every other dragon there's ever been. Once in every age, the first dragon laid an egg of its own and hid it for some foolish human to take home and hatch. And so our land became plagued with dragons. They attacked us and so they taught us hatred and warfare; they stole from us and hoarded what they stole so they taught us theft and greed; their breath brought disease and their fire brought famine – so the truly golden days were gone for ever.'

The friends got up without speaking and stood round the edges of the room, looking at the pictures in the floor. There was no doubt about it – they were telling the story that Zilla had just told. And maybe they'd been telling it for a thousand years. Maybe the story had already been ancient when the artist put it into the floor. The thought of all those centuries spiralling back to the beginning of the world made Ruel feel dizzy.

'Do you think there ever really *was* a time before the dragons?' he asked Zilla.

'It's hard to imagine, isn't it, dearie?' she said.

'Or to imagine a *future* without them,' Lexa added, quietly.

'Maybe that's why we've been finding it easier to think about fighting Abaddon than finishing off the dragons,' Ruel suggested.

Then another thought occurred to him – an answer to something that had been troubling him since their meeting with the villagers north of Mesaloth.

'Zilla,' he said, 'do you remember when Baladan said that the only way to finish off the dragons was to destroy their *root*? I couldn't work out what he meant but maybe it's got something to do with this story. Do you think Zethar's Great Dragon could be the dragon in the story – the one that made all the others?'

Zilla didn't get the chance to reply. A sudden clatter of hooves on stone turned everyone's attention to the cobbled roadway outside. It sounded eerie in this deserted place and for a moment they froze. But then they heard a shout from a familiar voice and all crowded to the doorway. The rain had stopped, the sun was out, and riding down the main street was Baladan on his faithful mount, Hesed. Baladan had a bow slung across his back, and the leather bags hanging on either side of Hesed were bulging with the results of his hunting. He had also, somehow, got hold of two more horses – they were following behind Hesed in single file.

'Ruel! Zilla!' Baladan called. 'Try out these horses! You have a journey to make.'

Often in these last weeks, Baladan had looked as sad and worn down as the rest of them but now there seemed to be a new energy – almost an excitement – in him and this, together with the change in the weather, seemed to lift everyone's spirits. Thassi and Chilion took the food away to prepare and the rest gathered round Ruel and Zilla and their horses. Only Zethar hung back, the heaviness of his task weighing on him – cutting him off from everyone as it had since the Tournament. He was certain that taking Baladan to the Great Dragon would be the death of their leader since Baladan was determined to meet the monster without an army to back him up. But still Zethar intended to complete his mission. It was a mission that had been given him by someone else, as well as Baladan. Disillusioned by Baladan's refusal to enter the Great Tournament, Zethar had had a secret meeting with Abaddon and had agreed to take Baladan to the Great Dragon so that it would destroy him and leave the way clear for Abaddon to lead an army against the monster. Zethar watched from a distance as his friends tried to get Zilla onto her horse. She was shrieking and laughing like a girl and the others were joining in her laughter. After a few moments, Zethar wandered away on his own into the empty streets.

No one in their village of Hazar had ever owned a horse but Zilla had ridden Hesed once when she'd gone with Baladan after The Dragon of Kiriath and Ruel had tried his hand at horsemanship when they'd all gone into training at Earl Rakath's castle a year ago. So neither of them was a complete novice but they still felt rather nervous when, a few minutes later, they set off with Baladan on their mystery journey.

'Don't worry,' he called to them, 'we're not going far but you need the horses. We have to move faster now. Things are happening – it's almost time.'

'Time for what?' Ruel asked.

But Baladan ignored the question. 'When you feel more comfortable, we'll trot,' he said. 'They're good horses – they'll do all the work for you. All you need is confidence.'

And it was true. After an hour, Ruel and Zilla felt sore but their anxiety had gone and Ruel had even galloped for a few minutes at Baladan's side – although how a knight could do that *and* manage his weapons at the same time remained a mystery to him. Towards the middle of the afternoon, Baladan brought them to a halt and pointed ahead.

'See anything?' he asked.

They'd been riding steadily east, which meant that the sun was now sinking behind them; and this made what Zilla and Ruel saw in front seem very strange. It was a glow, low in the sky, like a sunrise on the horizon.

'Will you gallop, Zilla?' Baladan asked.

And the three of them set off at full speed towards the light.

Soon they saw that the glow was flooding up from a deep valley some way ahead of them but the sides were so steep that it wasn't until they were at the valley rim that Ruel and Zilla could see what was in it. When they did, they saw that there was no *one* thing in the valley that was making the light – it was simply that *everything* down there was radiant. Somewhere at the back of his mind, Ruel thought that the sight should be hurting his eyes or dazzling him but instead he found that he could stare straight at the brightest object without the slightest discomfort.

The sides of the valley were grassy, and the grass was more brilliant than emeralds in sunlight. The valley bottom was covered with field after field of waving corn that could have been made of living gold and through the fields ran a river that sparkled like a stream of stars. The sound of the running water mixed with birdsong filled the air with a beautiful, gentle music that seemed to make Ruel's heart slow down and his whole body relax into the most wonderful feeling of peacefulness. There was perfume in the air too – the scent of flowers, perhaps – and Ruel found that he was taking such deep breaths that he thought he should be bursting but his lungs seemed big enough to breathe in for ever.

Ruel looked at Zilla, and saw that she too was breathing deeply, smiling as he'd never seen her smile before. There was something about how she was sitting, too – her chin was up, her shoulders back, and Ruel realised she looked much younger. Her hair was alive with colour – the glowing yellow that Zabad had once said she'd had as a young woman.

'Look at you!' said Ruel.

She turned to him and laughed.

'Look at *you*!' she replied.

They had no mirror, but Ruel looked at his hands and saw that they were big and strong, the backs of them dark with hair. He felt the hard muscles of his arms then ran his hands over his cheeks – they were rough with a man's stubble.

But Ruel couldn't keep his attention away from the valley

for long and soon he was pointing excitedly into the distance.

'What's that?' he asked Baladan.

The valley swept away eastwards to the sea and at the far end, Ruel had spotted something so dazzling that for a few moments it was impossible to make out its details. To begin with, it seemed like a huge diamond, surrounded by shifting sheets of soft white light. Then outlines began to become clear and Ruel made out fluttering flags – and walls, towers and turrets made of shining crystal.

'Do you remember,' Baladan said, quietly, 'the night we met – a dream you had?'

'The King's castle?' Ruel replied.

Baladan nodded. 'Is that better than your dream?' he asked.

'It's really real,' Zilla murmured. 'All my life, they called me mad for believing…'

'And you were right,' Baladan told her. 'You just never knew how right you were!'

Ruel and Zilla had both been gazing at the wonders down below. Now they looked towards their leader and what they saw made them blink in astonishment. Beside them was not a woodsman in cracked old leathers but a knight in full armour – and armour covered in gold at that. Crimson plumes cascaded from his helmet; he held a lance with a waving crimson pennant, and his horse was decked out in bright, coloured trappings of crimson and gold. He seemed to glow with the same radiance that was flooding out of the valley and if he had not had his visor raised, they would not have known that it was Baladan.

chapter four

'hat are you doing?' Baladan shouted.

Ruel had seen a track leading down the valley side and was walking his horse towards it.

'Aren't we going to the castle?' Ruel asked.

'No,' Baladan told him.

Ruel stopped in confusion.

'But aren't we going to get help?' he asked. 'Remember, when I had that dream – that was my quest. I was going to get help from the King – help to get rid of the dragons. It's been so long – so many things have happened – I'd given up hope. But now... we've *found* his castle, and you've got your armour – and there's the biggest dragon of them all to deal with – we *must* go for help!'

Baladan brought Hesed alongside Ruel and fixed the boy with his dark, steady eyes. The gold of his armour seemed to make a glow all around him.

'It's already been sent,' he said.

Then he turned Hesed's head and set off at an easy trot, back in the direction of the ancient fortress.

For a moment, Ruel didn't move. He felt immobilised by questions.

'Come on,' Zilla called. 'We'll never find our way back if we lose him.'

And they both turned their horses to follow Baladan.

'Wait!' Ruel shouted, as they started to close on him. 'What do you mean? What help? And your armour – how did that happen? What's going *on*?'

Baladan slowed Hesed to a walk, to let them catch up.

'Don't you know?' he asked Ruel, when they were beside

him again. 'Even *now*, can't you work it out?'

Ruel looked at Baladan, then behind him to where the light was still flooding up from the hidden valley, then back at Baladan again.

'*You're* it?' he said, at last. '*You're* the help from the King?'

'Yes, and more than yes,' Baladan told him.

Ruel's mouth went dry. 'The King's *son*?' he suggested, hesitantly. And when Baladan didn't reply, he added in a whisper, 'The *King*?'

Again, Baladan said nothing. He just smiled. Then he put a gauntleted finger to his lips.

'Don't tell anyone about this,' he said.

'Why not?' Ruel burst out, all the frustration of more than two years of this kind of mystery and secrecy bubbling over inside him. 'Why didn't you bring *everyone* here to see?' he demanded. 'It's all they want, to stop the arguing. If they could only see…' and he turned to point to the light over the valley – but it was gone.

He looked at Baladan, horrified, then pulled his horse's head round and galloped back towards the valley rim. He rode so hard that when he reached the edge, he had to wrench the reins to stop himself plunging over. The horse swerved and skidded on its haunches and Ruel stared in disbelief at the sight beneath him. The valley was dark, gloomy, filled with scrub and briars, and in the distance where it opened to the sea there was nothing – not even a ruin – to mark where the castle had been.

Then Ruel noticed his hands. They were thinner and the black hair had gone from the back of them. He felt his cheeks and there was no rasp of stubble – just the sparse wisps of a fourteen-year-old's first growth. He looked back towards Baladan and Zilla, a couple of hundred metres away, and there didn't seem to be any golden glow around their leader any longer. Ruel trotted back to them and sure enough, there was Baladan as he had always been, in his cracked leather jerkin, and Hesed had nothing but a saddle and the usual bags and bundles on his back. Zilla, too, was bent and grey, her cheeks sunken and wrinkled. But her eyes – her eyes were still shining with the wonder of what she'd seen.

'It's gone,' was all that Ruel could say.

'No,' Baladan told him. And there was such warmth and certainty in his voice that Ruel felt the despair that had risen up in him simply drain away. 'It's still there,' Baladan assured him, 'and more than there.'

'What do you mean?' Ruel asked.

'The King who owns that castle is king of more than this land,' Baladan told him. 'He's King of every kingdom there is – the King of all Kings – and so his castle must be in every kingdom there is.'

'I don't understand,' Ruel said.

'It can't be understood,' Baladan explained, 'only believed. Be thankful – you've seen something, a glimpse, to help you. I needed to show you, because I need you to keep believing in me. The hardest times are coming now – and the others will have to believe without seeing.'

'But why?'

'Because they can't. If they had come here with us, they would have seen nothing of what you two have seen. Then there would have been more arguments. You are the only two who are able to catch sight of the truth. And if you tell the rest what you've seen today, they won't believe you. You can't tell them anything about the valley – you can only show them what it's done for you – show them that you trust me. What I've asked of you all, all the time we've been together, is something as hard as facing a dragon – I've asked you to believe and trust in me. If you can do that, you'll have the strength for anything. You can tell them *that* when we get back, if you like.'

It was late afternoon by the time the three spotted the huge square of the fortress, a dark outline drawn on the dull greens and browns of the hillside. When they got back to the headquarters block, they saw smoke rising and found that a roaring fire was on the go and a meal had been prepared. The positive feeling the friends had caught from Baladan earlier in the day was still with them, and when they saw Ruel and Zilla, it got an extra boost. The pair seemed full of a new energy and the rest of them crowded round, pushing food into the travellers' hands – eager to know where they'd been and what they'd been up to. This was difficult, particularly since Ruel and Zilla were both desperate to tell what they'd seen but they didn't have to fend off questions for long. One of the twelve was missing – Thassi was on sentry duty – and just as Ruel was thinking he could at least risk saying they'd been to see a castle, the missing member burst into the room.

'Riders!' Thassi shouted, 'on the road from the west. Lots of them.'

At once, everyone sprang into action. Baladan had always refused to let them have weapons but they all instinctively found whatever they could to defend themselves. There were the sturdy branches that they'd brought for firewood, trimmed and stacked by the wall; Zethar snatched the one hatchet Baladan had let them have as a tool; Rizpa grabbed Baladan's bow from the corner of the room and Ruel had a hunting knife. The only person not caught up in the panic was Baladan. He continued to chew on the piece of meat he'd been given when he came in.

'They're friends,' he said, with his mouth full. 'I've been expecting them.'

By now they could hear the pounding of hooves – whoever was coming was riding hard. Then the rumble turned into the clattering of horseshoes on stone, and as they turned out into the gathering darkness, the friends saw that the road from the western gateway was full of mounted men. Moments later, the riders reached them in a whirl of snorting, stamping and the smell of sweating horses. There was a large open area opposite the headquarters block – perhaps it had been an exercise yard or a parade ground – and the horsemen drew themselves up there in good order, facing Baladan and his friends. They made three ranks each of about a dozen riders – just short of forty men. Their equipment looked businesslike – basic swords and shields but nothing more; many, but not all, had some kind of armour – just breastplates, and a few simple helmets.

No one but their leader had a full suit of armour – and it was a suit that Ruel recognised with shock. The leader of the war band sat easily in the saddle in front of his men and when the ranks were steady, he drew his battle sword, holding it up in a salute. Ruel recognised the sword too – he'd seen Baladan make it, as he'd seen him make the armour. Then the leader pushed up his visor, showing a hint of dark curls, a broad face and a firm gaze. There was no doubt about it now – the man was Jalam. Baladan's friends stared in amazement and someone gasped. The last time they'd seen Jalam, he'd been carried off the field of the Great Tournament on a stretcher – and he'd been stone cold dead.

But the questions they were desperate to ask were blocked. Jalam clearly had urgent news that could not wait for explanations.

'The Heights of Ataroth are taken,' he announced, without even dismounting. 'We've been trying to hold

Abaddon off since the Tournament but he's finally driven us out. We had war bands holding all the passes – but in the end he was too much for us. He's scattered our forces to the winds. We didn't know what to do apart from coming to find you.'

Without a word, Baladan stepped up to Jalam's stirrup and held out his arms to help the young man dismount. Jalam seemed exhausted and staggered as Baladan led him towards the headquarters. The other warriors lowered their aching bodies from their horses and together with Baladan's twelve, they crowded into the big room. There was a raised platform at one end where they found Baladan, Jalam at his side, waiting to address them.

'The crisis point has come,' Baladan told them. 'Abaddon has not spent so much time and spilt so much blood capturing the Heights of Ataroth for nothing. And so many brave warriors have not defended Ataroth this long without good reason.'

'He means to be crowned!' one of Jalam's band shouted.

'Indeed he does,' Baladan replied. 'The robber plans to be king – and it is on the Heights of Ataroth that the ancient rulers of the Old Kingdom have always been crowned. If there is to be a coronation, he knows it must be there and nowhere else.'

'We knew we had to keep him out,' Jalam said, desperation in his voice. 'Now he holds Ataroth, he will be crowned and that will be the end. No one will fight a crowned king. The war will be over and the Kingdom will be at his mercy.'

Glum murmuring broke out all round the room.

'No!' Baladan declared. 'He will *not* be King. Even though he has Ataroth, he will not be King.'

The muttering started again – full of confusion this time – until Jalam's voice rose above the rest.

'How can that be?' he asked.

'The coronation won't count – it won't be legal. It won't have *authority*,' Baladan explained. 'Only the King of Kings can give authority to make another king – in this or any land.'

At this, there was more puzzled conversation and Baladan looked intently at Ruel with an expression that seemed to say he expected *him* to understand even if nobody else did.

'There is a King above all kings,' Baladan went on, with a force that quietened everybody, 'and he gives authority to the king of every land. A messenger from this King of Kings must bring a sign of that authority for any coronation to be legal; and the new king must kneel before the messenger to show he recognises the authority of the King of Kings.'

'Try telling that to Abaddon!' one of the war band called out, with a hard laugh. 'What does he care about whether things are legal! He'll go ahead, messenger or no messenger – and the people won't know any different.'

Baladan glared at the man.

'Then we must tell them!' he said, in a voice full of emotion. 'There's still time. We must prevent this *mockery* of a coronation!'

And with that, Baladan jumped off the platform, pushed his way to the door and was gone into the darkness outside.

***

There was a moment of surprised silence then the room erupted into excited talk and the twelve rushed forward to gather round Jalam. They had something on their minds that, for the moment, seemed more important than any coronation – or even the sudden exit of their leader.

'We thought you were *dead*,' Ruel shouted, speaking for them all.

'You *were* dead,' Zilla added. 'We were *there*. We *saw* it. No one could have lived after a blow like that.'

'What happened?' Ruel asked.

Even his war band pressed close round Jalam when they heard this exchange – the suggestion that their leader had survived a mortal blow was clearly news to them.

'I don't know *what* happened,' Jalam told Ruel, 'and that's the honest truth. I remember beating Abaddon in the single combat to win the Tournament. And I remember taking my helmet off and saying that I wanted Baladan to be named Champion. Then a lot of arguing between the judges. Then nothing. It was only later that I found out how Abaddon had come up behind me and smashed my skull with his sword – but I don't remember anything about it. The next thing I remember after the judges arguing is that I was lying on something cold and hard and flat in complete darkness and someone was calling my name.

'I felt around and I realised I was lying on a stone slab. After a while, some strength seemed to start flowing back into my body and I managed to get up. The voice was still calling me. I thought it sounded like Baladan so I groped my way towards it. It was hard going because I was still in the dark, tripping over and knocking into things, but eventually I saw a dim light and made for that. I never did find the person who was calling me – the light was coming from a doorway and when I went though it, the voice stopped and there was no one in sight. I was in the open air and it was evening. I turned back to look at the doorway I'd just come through and I saw an inscription over the top – it was Earl Melech's family tomb.'

'So *were* you dead?' Ruel asked.

'*You* tell *me*,' Jalam replied. 'I really don't know. All I know is that I was standing outside that tomb and I was *alive* so I don't see how I *could* have been dead. But then again, Zilla says that after that blow from Abaddon, I *couldn't* have been alive.'

'What happened next?' Rizpa asked.

'I heard a whinny and when I looked, there was my horse, tethered to a tree. Not only that, all my armour was piled next to it, and my sword. Something told me it would be a good idea to be careful so I hid my things in the tomb and set off in search of anyone who could tell me what had happened since the Tournament had ended.

'The tomb was cut into the back of the hill with Earl Melech's castle on top. Round the other side was the plain where everyone had camped for the Tournament and there were still plenty of tents left so I realised I couldn't have been lying in the tomb all that long. There were campfires in amongst the tents so I wandered around, standing by groups of people as they were eating and drinking, listening to their conversations. Now and then, I'd risk asking someone a question but I always drifted off before anyone got too interested in me. Gradually I pieced together a picture of what had happened. It was four days since the Tournament and already the battle lines for the civil war had been drawn: Earl Jamin and Earl Rakath hadn't accepted Abaddon as Champion and had marched off south to their own lands with all their men, declaring their support for Baladan; but Earl Zafon and Earl Melech *had* accepted Abaddon and had given him command of their armies. In other words, as I was the person who'd actually beaten Abaddon and called for Baladan to be Champion, I was now in enemy territory – so it seemed like a good idea to keep my identity hidden and get out of there as quickly and quietly as I could.

'I made my way back to the tomb and was relieved to find that no one had taken my horse so I waited until nightfall, then armed myself and slipped away under cover of darkness.'

'How did you manage?' Zilla asked. 'Weren't you injured? I mean – your head – and that wasn't the only wound you got that day.'

'No,' Jalam told her. 'I was fine. It was strange but I didn't even feel tired. Lots of the people I'd heard talking round the campfires had been complaining about their wounds and bruises – some of them weren't expecting to be fit again for weeks – but I felt as if I'd never had a scratch.

'Something else I'd picked up round the campfires was that some of Earl Melech's men had deserted. They weren't for Abaddon and they'd gone into hiding, meaning to cause trouble for Abaddon if they could. I thought my best plan was to see if I could join up with one of these bands, and I got the chance a few days later. I was riding along a valley bottom one morning when I heard shouting and clanging steel up ahead and I knew there was a fight going on. I galloped towards it and found a couple of dozen men laying into each other in a small gorge off the main valley. One group had obviously ambushed the other and it wasn't hard to tell which were Abaddon's men. They were some of his personal riders with their studded leather jackets and short swords. So I shouted, "For Baladan!" and charged straight in. That seemed to tip the balance and Abaddon's men were soon sent packing.

'I joined the band and after a while, they did me the honour of choosing me as their leader.' He broke off for a moment to look at the battle-hardened group of warriors crammed into the room. 'Some of them are with me still,' he said, meeting the eyes of those who had fought beside him for the best part of half a year. 'We met up with several other bands over the following weeks and soon we had quite a force – enough to help defend the Heights of Ataroth.

We heard news that Abaddon was marching to take the place and I guessed his reason straight away. My father taught me all the ancient law of the land when I was only a boy and I knew that Ataroth was the hill of crowning. We joined with bands from all over the Kingdom who were defending the narrow passes that led to the Heights and they gave us news of other resistance groups scattered in every region. We heard Sir Achbor had a large force defending Kiriath and the villages round about – so Hazar and Maon are safe, as far as I know.'

The twelve were glad to hear that their villages were under Sir Achbor's protection but the news of Jalam's exploits stirred them up again with a desperate urge to get involved in the fight.

'The bands should all join together,' Chilion said, going back to his earlier idea.

'Exactly,' Jalam replied. 'Some of these groups are as big as battalions, if the reports are true. That's why we came searching for Baladan. Now that the Heights of Ataroth are lost we have to move fast. If Baladan raises his standard somewhere – calls us all together – I'm sure an army would gather that could do some real damage rather than just being a nuisance. Maybe we could even take back the Heights before it's too late. But we'll have to be quick. Make no mistake – if we don't stop that coronation, everything's lost. And if Abaddon wins the war, you can forget about clearing the Kingdom of dragons – he's got no interest in that job. All he wants is a king's right to dip his hands in every treasure chest in the land. He's no better than a dragon himself!'

Jalam's words about Abaddon and the dragons sent a chill through Zethar. He moved quietly away from his friends, and out of the building into the gathering gloom. It was all a matter of trust – did he trust Baladan or Abaddon to get rid of the Great Dragon? Everything Baladan did or said seemed to be madness whereas the way that Abaddon represented made perfect sense: meet force with force – meet the most powerful dragon in the land with the most powerful army in the land. But if Abaddon won the war, would he carry out his Champion's duty? *Would* he use the power of a conqueror – the army of a king – against the dragons?

Zethar found himself walking along the southern road beyond the fortress as he turned these questions over in his mind. The road didn't go very far – just up to the top of the hillside where it ended at a large tower. This tower looked out over the sea and had had a fire at the top in ancient times, to guide ships into the wide mouth of the river that flowed north of Mesaloth and reached the coast at this point. Now there was no fire, just blackened stone to show where the brazier had been – and the silhouette of a man, Baladan, staring out over the dark waters. Zethar watched Baladan surveying the waters and willed him to go back to the fortress and take command of Jalam's band – to defeat Abaddon and take control of the Grand Army – to turn his back on his mad idea of meeting the Great Dragon alone.

By the time Baladan returned to the headquarters, Zethar had already slipped back in and was attending to the discussion between the rest of the twelve and Jalam about drawing together an army to fight against Abaddon. They had pooled the knowledge of the Old Kingdom they'd gained in their travels and had worked out where best to gather their forces; Jalam had given all the information he had about where different bands of supporters were operating. The whole idea had become very real to them and when Baladan came in, Jalam jumped up to meet him, full of enthusiasm. He brought Baladan towards the fire and outlined the plan in all its detail. It culminated in a major attack on Abaddon to prevent his coronation.

'There's only one thing we need,' Jalam finished. 'We need you to lead us.'

Zethar held his breath.

Baladan looked at Jalam for a long time and remembered. He remembered how he'd first met this fearless young warrior at his father's tiny, broken down fort on the western borders; how desperate the young man had been to fight in the Tournament; how he'd kitted Jalam out and trained him; how Jalam had taken on all comers to become the rightful Champion then had tried to give the title away to his teacher. Baladan looked at the strong, honest face of Jalam and was filled with love and admiration for him.

They made a powerful contrast as they stood together in the firelight: Jalam still wore his breastplate and a dagger hung at his belt – every inch a soldier at the ready; Baladan stood unarmed in the old, cracked leather jerkin he always wore, looking like nothing more than a common woodsman.

'If you want to follow me,' Baladan said, at last, 'you must leave your weapons and your armour here.'

He said it gently, with no hint of accusation, and Jalam continued to look at Baladan for a moment longer before he dropped his gaze to stare uncomfortably at the floor. The weight of disappointment seemed to make the young soldier's body shrink.

'I left myself unprotected once before,' he said. 'I will never do it again.'

Baladan put his hand on Jalam's shoulder.

'In that case,' he told him, 'you must take your men and whoever else you can gather and defend the south. The city of Mesaloth is sure to have been captured by now and it won't be long before the castle falls. After that, Oreb will want to clear any resistance in the forest then march against Earl Jamin. And if he defeats Jamin, he can simply seal Earl Rakath off in his castle by the sea and leave him to rot. Oreb must *not* get the better of the southern earls – your job is to hold him up as long as possible. But you must leave "Earl" Abaddon and his coronation to me.'

CHAPTER FIVE

*A*fter the injury to Nara's ankle, Aia had taken her to a hideout not far from the pit she'd fallen into and allowed her to rest, under guard, for the remainder of the day. He'd ordered Penina to bandage their captive's ankle with some special leaves, which had helped a little with the swelling. Nara had been right about the gang having reserves of food so she'd eaten, too, before they'd tied her up for the night. But next morning, Aia didn't show any signs of taking up the offer Nara had made to fight him once she was fed and rested. Instead, he had her untied and led her with the rest of his band on a trek through the forest.

Her ankle was still very sore, and if it hadn't been for that, Nara was sure she could have escaped. That is, if she'd wanted to. But she had a very good reason for *not* wanting to get away, even if she'd been fit: it was obvious to her that Aia's band could survive in the forest and equally obvious that on her own, she could not. So Nara decided to keep quiet and await developments as they wove their way between the trees. But she didn't stay silent for long. They quickly returned to the stream she'd followed out of Mesaloth the day before and started to follow its course – but they were going *with* the current. When she realised this, Nara had sudden doubts.

'Hey!' she shouted to Aia. 'This is going to lead us to Mesaloth!'

'Exactly,' he called back, without turning.

'But Abaddon's men are there,' she went on.

'That's right,' he replied.

His calm increased her unease.

'Why are you taking me there?' she asked.

'We're after their food,' Aia told her, 'since you spoiled our hunting yesterday – *and* polished off a fair bit of our reserves.'

'That's crazy,' Nara said.

He didn't reply.

'We often raid their camp,' Penina explained, quietly.

She was marching beside Nara, with an arm round her waist to support her and Nara was thankful – she was leaning hard on the girl's shoulder as she limped along.

'But they've moved *inside* Mesaloth now,' Nara told her. 'They've gone *inside*,' she shouted ahead to Aia. 'All their stores will be in the city. It fell two days ago.'

'I know,' Aia replied. 'That's why we're taking you. If you come from Mesaloth, you'll know your way around. I think you owe us something, don't you?'

Nara wasn't at all sure that she owed them *anything* – it was the other way round, as far as she was concerned – but she weighed up the likelihood of survival in a raid on the city with survival on her own in the forest and decided she might at least earn a place in the gang if she stuck with them now.

Soon they left the bank of the stream and struck off through the dense mass of trees. Every trunk looked the same to Nara and they might have been going round in circles for all she could tell but Aia clearly knew his way. The stream took a winding course but the gang was going in as straight a line as the trees allowed, and Mesaloth was in sight again in a surprisingly short time. Following the stream to get away from the city had been logical but not very efficient, Nara realised. Aia got his band established in a position well out of sight, with a good view of the city gates, then he settled down to watch and wait. Nara's hopes of success grew: whatever Aia was going to do, it clearly wouldn't be done in haste.

Yesterday's torrential rain had delayed things but now,

halfway through the second morning since the city fell, the clear-up operations after the battle for Mesaloth were well under way. Nara noticed that all the siege towers had been moved away from the walls so she couldn't suggest using them as a route in and out. The city gates were permanently open, though, as wagons were passing through all the time – but so were squads of soldiers. There was plenty of bustle to provide cover but it was dangerous bustle. After watching the comings and goings for about half an hour, Aia beckoned his band close to him and outlined his plan.

'Those wagons have got such high sides, no one can see what's in them from the ground,' he said. 'They're our way in and out. The ones going in are coming from what's left of their old camp. If we can climb into one of them when it's been loaded up, it'll take us straight into the city. We'll have to get out again, without being noticed, of course, and we don't know what's going on inside the walls but we'll just have to take a chance on that. When we're in, Nara can help us hunt down their stores and keep hidden until we've worked out how to get on board one of the wagons coming back.'

It was far from foolproof but if they were going to go ahead, it seemed to Nara the only possible way to enter and leave the city unseen.

The besieging army's old camp was to their left and Aia's band crept cautiously towards it, under cover of the trees.

'We have to be careful,' Penina whispered to Nara. 'The soldiers often come into the forest to hunt. That's why we have to steal their food – they've hunted so much that there's hardly anything left for us. To be honest, I don't think we had much chance of catching anything in that pit you fell into, anyway.'

'Keep *quiet*, Penina!' Aia hissed.

They continued in silence but as it happened, they didn't

have anything to worry about from wandering parties of soldiers or even guards at the camp. Everyone was fully occupied dismantling things and loading up the wagons: it had been a huge camp and would take several days to clear, even with everyone working flat out. When they got within spying distance, the raiders spotted a group of four wagons at the edge of the camp area, obviously loaded and ready to go. The wagoners were gathered round a quartermaster about fifty metres away, arguing over some entry that had to be made in the records and there were no spare soldiers to stand guard.

'There's our ride,' Aia whispered.

He'd picked five gang members, including Nara, to go with him and now he led them in a crouching run across to the big wooden vehicles. Nara came in last, sweating and cursing with pain. They slid under the nearest wagon and hid for a moment behind its huge solid wheels, making sure they hadn't been seen. The wagons were standing in pairs so one side of each was shielded from view by its neighbour. One at a time, the raiders climbed this hidden side of their wagon and dropped silently into it. Limping through the forest then having to run for the wagon had been painful enough for Nara with her injury but the jarring as she landed made her bite her lip to stop a yelp. She lay still for some time, clutching her ankle with her eyes screwed tight shut against the pain. She could see stars behind her eyelids and waves of nausea swept over her.

It was only when the wagon was jolted into motion that Nara felt able to look around. Her eyes were blurred with tears and she felt dizzy so it took a moment for her to focus but when she did, she saw they'd landed among a cargo of wooden barrels. She put her ear to one of them and hit it several times with her fist.

'Quiet!' Aia hissed, tugging her sleeve furiously.

'Do you think anyone is going to hear that?' she replied, hardly bothering to lower her voice.

The heavy wagon was rumbling like thunder and it was obvious that her knocking would have been completely lost in the din.

'It's not drink in there,' Nara said. 'It sounded solid. I think we might have hit the bull's-eye.'

'What do you mean?' Aia asked.

'I mean, if it's not wine or beer, there's only one other thing that's likely to be packed in barrels. I bet we've jumped right into a load from their food store. Let's see if we can get the top off one of them.'

They searched for something to use and Aia soon found a hooked metal bar in the bottom of the wagon. The wagoner must have thrown it in for just the job Nara had in mind and Aia soon prised off one of the tops. When he did, he smiled at Nara and slapped her hand: she was right – it *was* food. The barrel was packed with salted meat.

'Good,' Aia said. 'That saves us having to search the city.'

'A pity the wagon set off so soon,' Nara commented. 'We could have loaded ourselves up and got straight out again.'

'Well, loading up's a good idea, anyway,' Aia replied, 'then we can try and get out as soon as it stops. If it's still outside the walls, it'll save us having to steal another ride.'

So all of them stuffed their clothes with as many pieces of meat as they could manage and waited for the wagon to come to a halt.

'My foot still hurts a lot,' Nara said, after a while.

'So?' Aia replied.

'So I can't run very far – when we get out, I mean.'

Nara wasn't asking for sympathy. It was a plain statement of fact. If their escape was going to mean a long dash to safety, she'd be done for. Aia met her eyes with a hard stare.

'If there's trouble, there'll be no going back for people,

no heroic rescues,' he told her. 'You'll just have to take your chances. Don't expect anything from any of us.'

⟨ornament⟩

The wagons were roughly made and they could spy through the gaps between the boards. The first stop was at the city gates and it was clear straight away that it would be madness for any of them to get out there. Soldiers were everywhere and no matter how fast they ran, none of the gang could have safely made the five-hundred-metre dash back to the trees.

'If we don't get out before this thing arrives at the storehouse, we've got a problem,' Aia said. 'They'll probably start unloading straight away. If that happens, we'll just have to scatter and hope for the best.'

He looked at Nara without any hint of feeling and she stared blankly back. With her injury, she wouldn't be scattering very far and they both knew it.

There was some shouting from the guards then someone banged on the wagon side; the heavy wooden wheels started rolling again and in another moment, Nara was back in the city of Mesaloth. Straight away her mind got to work on the possibilities. She pressed her eye to a gap in the wagon side and tried to work out where they were going and where the conquerors might have set up their stores. It seemed likely to her that they'd have taken over some of the city's own storehouses: there was nothing else in them, after all, thanks to the siege. The wagon certainly seemed to be heading in that direction. As she was considering this, they stopped again and a lot of angry shouting broke out ahead. They could see through the boards that they'd come to a halt in a narrow street but they couldn't tell what was going on. Aia climbed cautiously onto the barrels until he could see where the shouting was coming from then dropped back down at once.

'Quick!' he whispered. 'Everyone over the back!'

A wagon coming the other way along the street had caused a jam ahead and the drivers were arguing. The wagon the raiders were hiding in was the final one in the convoy and if they moved fast, it looked to Aia as if no one would see them.

Nara was last out of the wagon and when she got ready to drop to the street, she saw Aia waiting below to catch her. She flopped down against his chest and he clutched her, staggering as he tried to save her from landing with her full weight on her injured ankle.

'I don't want you damaged any more,' he explained. 'I need you to get us back to the gates.'

'Sure,' she said, wriggling free and limping to the doorway where she could see the others hiding.

They lay low for a few minutes until the wagoners had sorted themselves out and cleared the street then they set out for the gates with Nara in the lead.

It was only a day and a half since she'd last made her way through the captured city but already much of the debris that had given her shelter had been cleared. And most of the bodies were gone now, too. All this made the journey to the gates much more hazardous that Nara's previous escape and on top of that, it was daylight and there were many more soldiers about. Nara's ankle wasn't such a liability though, as none of the raiders was moving very quickly. It was painstaking work, slipping from one abandoned house to another, sometimes waiting several minutes until the way was clear to move on again.

But they were making steady progress and everyone was feeling encouraged – everyone except for Nara. Something was worrying her.

'We're getting too near the city gates,' she whispered to Aia, when they were within a few streets of their target.

'What do you mean?' he asked.

'We can't get too near the gates,' she explained. 'There's a big barracks there. It'll be crowded with soldiers.'

'All right,' Aia said. 'Time to pick up another ride.'

<hr/>

Half an hour later, the six raiders slipped out of the shelter of a narrow alley and crawled under the thick canvas cover of a stationary wagon. It was a different design from the one that had carried them into Mesaloth – slightly smaller with an open back – and it had come to a halt because a big charred roof beam was blocking the street. Aia had identified this street as one that wagons were using every few minutes to reach the gates; and while the street had been empty, he'd organised his followers to heave the beam across it. By the time the wagoner had got help and shifted the beam, all six raiders were well hidden under the canvas. It was completely dark under there and they couldn't see what cargo they were lying on, but it was very lumpy and uncomfortable and smelt revolting. Nara felt around for a moment to investigate then took a sharp breath. Her fingers had closed on an ice-cold, rigid hand.

'It's bodies,' she hissed.

Once it was outside the city, the wagon left the track and bumped over rough ground for some time before it finally came to a halt. The wagoner pulled off the canvas cover and found only what he expected – a pile of blue-grey, naked corpses. He went to the back of the wagon, muttering and cursing his luck for being given such a disgusting job. It was his fifth trip of the day so far and he was exhausted, fed up and getting more rather than less on edge with each load of carcasses. The bodies made some horrible noises as air escaped from them and occasionally one of the limbs would jerk. The wagoner braced himself and took hold of the nearest body. He hauled it off by the ankles and let it drop into the huge pit where he'd backed up his wagon. It was one of four. The other three were already full. This latest body landed on a pile already several metres deep, scattering a flock of crows into the air. It slithered, rolled over and lay still.

The wagoner rubbed his aching shoulders and turned back for the next body. But as he gripped its ankles and got ready to heave, a sound came from the wagon like nothing he'd ever heard since he'd started this gruesome job – it was an eerie wailing and it went on for several seconds. He let go of the body he was holding and instinctively looked around, as if the noise might have come from someone or something other than his grisly load – but he was completely alone. He looked back at his wagon and to his horror, he saw that the bodies in the middle seemed to be heaving. Suddenly an arm shot out, then another, and finally the complete naked torso of a young man jerked upright, staring, wide-eyed, straight at the wagoner. Then, with an open, gaping mouth, it screamed. That was enough for the poor man. He screamed, too, and without looking back, set off running towards the city at top speed.

As soon as the wagoner was gone, the screaming 'corpse' dragged himself clear of the bodies on the wagon. He was stripped only to the waist and reached down between the cold arms and legs where he'd been hiding to retrieve the rest of his clothes and a sizeable quantity of stolen meat.

'All clear,' he said.

As their leader dressed again, the other five raiders struggled out from the heap of bodies where they'd burrowed during their journey out of Mesaloth. They stood for a moment in appalled silence, looking almost as pale as the countless corpses that surrounded them, then Aia led them away towards the forest.

The grave pits had been dug quite a way to the west of the city and it took the six raiders some time to work their way back, under cover of the forest fringe, to the place where the rest of the gang was hiding. Aia had left the youngest children behind and they had been getting more and more anxious as they waited for the raiding party to return. They'd been left in good cover in a tiny dell near the edge of the forest and as long as they kept still and quiet, they'd be safe; but Penina, in particular, had become increasingly restless as time wore on with no sign of the others coming back. At eight, she was far from being the youngest but seemed the most fretful. Time after time, she crept to the edge of the dell to look out for the raiders returning, despite the rest of the youngsters begging her to keep still, in case she gave them away. After all, they weren't very far from all the activity at the old army camp and there were still plenty of Abaddon's soldiers coming and going.

Aia and his group were well aware of that, too, and as they got nearer to the place where they'd left the youngsters, they moved with increasing care. Nara was exhausted with pain by now and the slow, creeping pace was a relief; but she could tell that the others were eager to be moving faster. They were clearly longing to get out of the danger zone as quickly as possible and back to comparative safety in the depths of the forest. Perhaps this impatience or tiredness made them less alert – but whatever the reason, as they approached the dell, they failed to notice a small patrol of soldiers moving out of the old camp in the direction of the trees.

The raiders were still keeping themselves well hidden, though. They were quite near to the dell before Penina, on the look out again, saw some movement in the undergrowth and caught a glimpse of the green jacket that she knew was Nara's. She'd taken a strong liking to this brave newcomer and had been more anxious about *her* not returning from the raid than about anyone else. As soon as she saw that flash of green, Penina jumped to her feet.

'Nara!' she yelled, and set off running towards her, crashing through any bushes in her way.

Aia dashed to meet her in alarm.

'Shut *up*, Penina!' he whispered urgently, clapping his hand over her mouth and holding her still.

All the others froze, held their breath and listened.

Only five hundred metres away, ten of General Oreb's soldiers stood frozen, too. Then their officer pointed and beckoned, and the patrol began to edge slowly and silently in the direction of the sounds they'd heard.

After a moment or two, Aia let go of Penina. He held his fingers to his lips and glaring at her, led his party back to the others in the dell. Now that she realised the danger she'd put them all in, Penina was tearful and when she grabbed Nara round the waist, it was for comfort rather than to support her new friend. But Nara was thankful for this sturdy little body to lean on again, and as they moved off, clinging to each other for their different reasons, she began to feel towards Penina the way she'd felt for the group of orphans she'd tried to look after in the chaos of Mesaloth under siege. Penina looked up at her and Nara used her finger to wipe away the two big tears hanging under the child's eyes.

Half an hour later, Aia seemed to think that they were well clear of danger and he ordered a halt.

'Let's see what we've got,' he said, and those who had been to Mesaloth dug into their baggy clothes, pulling out enough pieces of meat to keep the whole gang going for a week.

'Does that make up for spoiling our pit?' Penina asked, pointing at the four sizeable cuts that Nara had taken from underneath her jacket.

'I suppose so,' Aia replied, and he turned to Nara. 'We release you,' he told her. 'You can go now, if you want to.'

Nara was just working out how best to ask if she could stay when there was a strange whistle and a thump and Aia staggered backwards, clutching his thigh. Half a metre of arrow shaft was sticking out between his fingers.

'Run!' he shouted, as another arrow whistled past, this time bouncing harmlessly off a tree trunk.

They all took off in the opposite direction to the one the arrows had come from and now they could hear shouting and the sound of men crashing through the undergrowth in pursuit. Nara snatched a glance behind and saw the soldiers of General Oreb's patrol closing in fast on their injured leader. She was moving slowly enough herself but the arrow in his leg made escape impossible for Aia.

The panic-stricken dash away from their attackers went on for some minutes before Nara called out to the gang to stop. All except Penina were well ahead of her by now but her voice was commanding and, one by one, they came back.

'I think they've given up,' Nara panted.

They listened anxiously for several moments but at last they agreed – there were no more sounds of the chase. Neither was there any sign of their leader. Perhaps the soldiers were satisfied with one victim and the hoard of meat, most of which had been left on the ground when they'd fled.

'We could go back for Aia,' Nara said. 'There weren't many of them. I'm sure we could rescue him. He wasn't badly wounded.'

She looked from one face to another but none of them showed the least desire to save their leader.

'We never go back for people,' Penina explained softly. 'It's everyone for themself.'

CHAPTER SIX

he place that was known as the Heights of Ataroth – the ancient site on which tradition demanded all rulers of the Old Kingdom should be crowned – was a hill. But this was no ordinary hill. It wasn't natural. It had been *made* by human hands. No one could tell how long ago it was that an army of labourers had sweated and groaned to raise the huge mound of earth but everyone was agreed that the Heights of Ataroth represented the oldest mark that human beings had made on this land. And it was an awesome mark, giving rise to legends that the first inhabitants of the Old Kingdom had been giants. As the sun rose over the hill on the morning of Abaddon's coronation day, it *looked* like a giant, asleep under a thick blanket of grass. The top was a level oval, a kilometre long by half a kilometre wide, and its sides curved down to the surrounding plain, thirty metres below. But this monster of a mound wasn't the end of those ancient labourers' work. It was surrounded by three great oval ramparts made of piled-up earth, one inside the other with deep ditches in between, looking like the rumpled folds of the giant's blanket.

These earth walls were Ataroth's defences. No one knew when soldiers had last patrolled them before Abaddon's arrival but the walls didn't need a garrison to be effective in defending the Heights. Something about the whole place made people very reluctant to go beyond those looming ramparts, even when they were deserted: twenty men had had to be whipped as an example to the rest before one of Abaddon's battalions could be persuaded to go through the gateway gap at the southern end and clear the Heights for the coming ceremony. The place had been unused for over a generation – so long that the whole site was overgrown with a thick tangle of bushes and brambles. There were even clumps of trees that had rooted and grown to a considerable height. None of this would do for Abaddon – his coronation was not going to be some shoddy business hurried through in a mess of undergrowth. So in the six weeks since the robber's forces had taken control of the area, the Heights of Ataroth had been the scene of constant chopping, hacking and dragging, until now at last, the mound lay ready in the early light of a fine March morning – a smooth green outline against a pale pink sky.

Half a kilometre to the south the people of the town of Migdal were just waking up. It was going to be a big day for them – many of the merchants were hoping to make their fortune during the course of the coronation celebrations, as all the tavern owners already *had* done by providing hospitality for Abaddon's men in the run-up to the grand occasion. Whether they supported Abaddon or not, the people of Migdal certainly liked the trade he'd brought to their town. But the great man himself – the Grand Champion, the Earl of the Middle Lands, the King-to-be – was not in Migdal. He and his chief officers and advisers were camped to the north of the town on the plain between Migdal and the Heights, in magnificent tents of yellow silk, all fluttering with the red flags that bore the emblem of Abaddon – a gold crown and sword. A wooden palisade had been built round these silk palaces and outside it was camped a brigade of Abaddon's best troops – men who'd been with him since the days when he was no more than a savage bandit, terrorising the heartland of the Old Kingdom.

Before dawn broke on the morning of his coronation day, Abaddon had already been awake for what seemed to him like hours but it wasn't excitement and the anticipation of his final triumph that had driven him out of bed. It was worry. He'd dressed in the dark – not in the clothes he was to wear for the ceremony but in his old, studded leather fighting gear. He'd buckled on his sword and strode purposefully out of the compound. Guards had stepped forward to challenge him then melted back into the shadows without a word – even in the dim light before dawn, there had been no mistaking the huge frame of their leader. He was a head taller than anyone in his army and built like a bull.

As the sky became paler and dawn approached, Abaddon marched towards the Heights of Ataroth. Whenever he was anxious – which wasn't often – activity was his answer. He pushed himself on at the double, through the gap in the earth ramparts and up the side of the mound. It was steeper than it seemed from a distance and by the time he reached the great oval at the top, he was soaked with sweat, his barrel chest heaving for breath.

The whole space on top of the mound was empty. Not even the Crowning Stone was there. Later that morning it would be carried up from the fortified tower in the middle of Migdal where it was kept, at the head of the grand procession of all who would gather on the mound to see a thief crowned King. But for now the thief was alone. As the dawn light crept over the Heights of Ataroth, Abaddon stood, panting and perspiring, to greet the sun. He spread his arms wide, threw his head back and roared – a great battle roar that could send hardened soldiers running without a blow being struck. But strangely, something in the quality of the air on the Heights seemed to smother the sound. And the sun had no warmth in it for Abaddon:

cold sweat trickled down his back and made him shiver. Big though he was, when his servants reported him missing and an anxious search began, no one spotted him on top of the Heights of Ataroth, and his roar was silenced by distance: in his camp, nothing could be heard except the twittering of the early morning birds and nothing seen but the strange, smooth shape of the mound and an empty plain.

Abaddon scattered men on either side of him like chickens when he eventually returned to his camp. A flock of fussing officers and advisers rushed out to meet him when he was sighted at last, striding towards the tents, but they fell back quickly when they saw the furious glowering in his face. Those that weren't quick enough in getting out of the way were shoved so hard they tumbled.

'Where's Zemira?' Abaddon bellowed. 'Send me Zemira!' and he marched on to his tent, ripping the fine silk as he pulled the flap aside.

Zemira was a young lord with flowing brilliant orange hair, long delicate fingers and a deep knowledge of the ancient laws of chivalry and kingship but not much else. He was also a superb musician and composer of songs. Those long fingers could make his harp sound like everything bright and beautiful in the whole world gathered into one tumbling crystal cascade. But it wasn't for the beauty of his music that Abaddon wanted Lord Zemira now – the chink of money and the clash of swords were the only music he enjoyed – it was for the *words* of a song he'd written.

'Sing it again!' Abaddon ordered, when Lord Zemira came hurrying into the tent.

'I'll get my harp,' he said, half turning to go.

'Never mind that – just sing!' Abaddon barked.

The song Abaddon wanted to hear was a long one, in an ancient traditional form. It was a 'King Song' – the kind of song always sung at the crowning of a new monarch, so Lord Zemira had told Abaddon when they had planned the coronation ceremony together. A 'King Song' was intended to tell the story of the new king's ancestry and was a kind of proof that he was entitled to the crown. Abaddon settled back in the carved wooden throne that had been installed in his tent to hear once more the 'King Song' Lord Zemira had written for him. He had listened to it often enough in the last few days but it seemed vital this morning to hear it again and to *believe* it. Abaddon had stolen many things in his time but standing alone at dawn on the Heights of Ataroth had confirmed what he had known deep down for weeks – that taking the crown of the Old Kingdom was theft on a different level altogether.

Abaddon's 'King Song' was, of course, a pack of lies – but they were Abaddon's lies, not Zemira's. The robber had been deceiving the young lord about his ancestors ever since he'd persuaded him to join his side at the Great Tournament last autumn. Zemira was no good at fighting, but he *did* have piles of money and Abaddon never passed up the chance to get his hands on treasure. However, he'd realised that the chivalrous lord would never support a low-born robber such as himself, so he'd told Zemira that he wasn't really a swineherd's son, as everyone thought, but a member of a noble family who'd had his inheritance stolen by sorcery. This was the kind of romantic story Lord Zemira loved to hear and he'd lapped it up.

Once Abaddon had decided to take the crown, all that was needed to convert this piece of nonsense into a 'King Song' was to make out that the 'noble family' he came from was actually a branch of the old *royal* family of the Kingdom.

The robber was glaring at Zemira so fiercely that the young lord's throat was drained of moisture. He swallowed hard, coughed several times, then began:

'Who sings of the sun, the sky's brightest treasure,
Or tells of the tempest – that torrent of power?
My words paint more wealth, more wondrous strength
Than the heavens can hold. I hail Abaddon!'

As Zemira got into his stride, he threw his head back, closed his eyes, and sang the song with beauty and passion. The beauty left Abaddon untouched but he caught the passion. The young man really looked as if he *believed* what he had written and was singing – as if he truly believed that Abaddon was the rightful king. Abaddon felt himself hanging on to Zemira's passionate belief like a dangling climber clinging to a rope. It was crazy, but deep inside himself, Abaddon felt that he *had* to believe he had a right to be king or he was lost. How or why he could be lost he couldn't tell: everywhere his armies went, they were carrying the field; he'd just heard that the castle at Mesaloth had fallen a week ago – surely nothing could stop him now. But still he was nagged by doubt.

'Good! Good!' Abaddon declared, when Zemira had done. 'Now go through the arrangements again.'

Abaddon had suggested to Zemira that since he like the old traditions so much, he might like to pay for the expenses of the coronation. To his surprise, the young man had paid up without any pressure and had even said that he was *honoured*. Then Zemira had said he had all the ancient details of how a coronation should take place and would be happy to advise. Abaddon had seized on this. Something instinctive had told him that if nothing else was right, at least he had to get the *details* of the ceremony spot on. So Lord

Zemira had been put in charge of all arrangements and once again, he explained them now to Abaddon.

The robber hunched his bulk on the edge of his seat, creasing his big face with concentration. All his life, he'd smashed anything in his way to get what he wanted and now it was hard to give attention to tiny particulars – who should wear what, who should sit where, who should say what to whom and in which order – but he was determined to get everything right and had become almost as obsessive as Zemira.

There were some things they couldn't get right, though, the most important being the authority from the King of Kings. Abaddon, along with most people in the Old Kingdom, had never heard of this King of Kings – but there it was in the ancient texts which Zemira had been escorted to his castle to fetch: 'a messenger from the King of Kings must bring authority for the crowning'.

'Get the old fool in here,' Abaddon barked, when Zemira reached that bit of the plans. 'I'm not taking any chances with him messing things up.'

Zemira immediately knew who Abaddon meant and went in search of Sir Shamma. He came back a moment later with a thin, stooped old man, whose wrinkled face was almost hidden in a cascade of white hair. He was not really a 'Sir' at all, just an old eccentric who lived in a fantasy world of knights and damsels in distress. Lord Zemira had run into him on his way to the Great Tournament and taken him under his wing. They had been together ever since, and Abaddon had realised that the old man would be perfect casting for the part of 'messenger from the King'. He'd believe he was anyone they told him he was as long as it had to do with chivalry – it was just a question of whether he'd remember what to do.

'My Lord Messenger,' Zemira said to Shamma, going

through the lines that had to be spoken, 'what news from the King of Kings?'

Shamma drew himself up as straight as he could.

'The King of all Kings sends greetings to his servant, Earl Abaddon!' the old man proclaimed.

There was a pause and Lord Zemira looked meaningfully at Abaddon. Abaddon glared back and shook his head.

'If we don't do it all, he might not get it right later on,' Zemira whispered anxiously.

Abaddon swore under his breath then laboriously got down on his knees before the old man.

'Do you, Earl Abaddon of the Middle Lands, pay homage to The Lord, The King of Kings; and do you promise faithfully to do his bidding and uphold his laws in ruling the kingdom he gives you?' Sir Shamma asked, his voice unusually firm and loud.

'I do,' Abaddon muttered.

Another pause.

'He didn't hear you,' Zemira hissed.

'*I do!*' Abaddon shouted, furiously.

Sir Shamma placed a shaking hand on Abaddon's head.

'Then receive the authority of the King of Kings,' the old man declared, 'and rise – *King* Abaddon.'

Abaddon sprang up – with remarkable speed for such a big man – and turning his back on Shamma, he stalked to the other end of the tent.

'Get him out!' he snarled.

When Zemira had ushered Sir Shamma away, he turned back to find Abaddon staring at his coronation robes, hanging on a stuffed dummy. Zemira came to his side and they stood for a moment in silence before the straw figure in royal robes, both preoccupied with their own misgivings. The young lord may have been taken in by Abaddon's made-up ancestry, but there was no way that even Abaddon could pretend to him that Shamma was anything other than a fraud. However, Zemira's longing to *witness* the crowning of a king was incredibly strong. And, of course, there was also the question of the horrible death Abaddon had promised him if he gave so much as a hint that all was not as it should be with the coronation.

There was something else that was going to be missing from the coronation and, unlike the messenger from the King of Kings, it was something that *everyone* knew about. It was being argued over later that morning in the silk tent next to Abaddon's. This was the tent that had been allocated to the two Great Earls who would support Abaddon at his coronation – Earl Zafon of the North and Earl Melech of the East. The problem was that the tent should have housed *four* Great Earls.

'You can argue all morning, Zafon,' Earl Melech was saying, 'the whole Kingdom knows that all *four* of the Earls must support a new king. If there are only two of us, the crowning *will not* unite the Kingdom. Don't you see, the coronation will just reinforce what we are – a divided land: two against two; two here, two not; a Kingdom at war with itself. What kind of a way is *that* to make a king?'

'The *only* way, in the present circumstances, I suggest,' Earl Zafon replied, smoothly. 'Abaddon's *strength* is what this Kingdom needs, not two more Earls at a coronation. Sometimes rules have to be bent, for everyone's good – *you* should know that as well as anyone.'

Earl Melech looked away. He didn't need Zafon to spell out what he was referring to. Last autumn, Earl Melech had given the Champion's crown to Abaddon at the Tournament he'd hosted, when it was clear to everyone that the robber had cheated. Earl Melech had done so with a ring of Abaddon's armed riders surrounding him and had told himself he had no choice; just as he'd told himself he had no choice but to support Abaddon in the civil war that had followed and at this mockery of a coronation. But the excuse didn't make him feel any happier with the way he'd acted or the way things were turning out.

'It's only a matter of time, anyway,' Zafon went on. 'Now that the castle's fallen at Mesaloth, General Oreb will be mopping up resistance. Anyone left in the forest, whoever they are, will be driven out. It won't be long before he's burning every village from there to the coast and then he'll take Earl Jamin. There'll soon be a third earl to kneel at Abaddon's feet, don't you worry!'

'And what about Earl Rakath?' Melech persisted.

'The man's a buffoon,' Zafon said with a laugh. 'He can't stand alone – he'll be with us too, in the end. I tell you – it's only a question of time.'

'Then why not wait?' Melech asked.

'We need a king *now*,' Zafon insisted. 'It will unite the country – no one will fight their crowned king. It'll end the war – it'll save lives!'

Zafon's thin mouth was smiling but the narrow, dark eyes above his sharp nose were glittering with menace. Earl Melech had never trusted his northern neighbour, and the experience of being his ally in this war had not improved his opinion of the man.

Further argument was cut short by the blare of trumpets outside. Both the Earls knew what this meant. The morning was wearing on and the grand procession to the Heights of Ataroth was being called to order. The two men stared at each other for a moment – Zafon still smiling, Melech exasperated but resigned – then they turned to their own ends of the tent and finished putting on their robes. A few moments later, they left together, marching side by side with the solemn expressions befitting their noble rank and the magnitude of the occasion.

The procession was a magnificent sight. At its head was a platoon of guards from Migdal, in ceremonial golden armour, the like of which no one had ever seen before. A dozen sets had been found in store in the ancient tower of Migdal, and days had been spent polishing them up. Crimson velvet cloaks and leggings had also been found but they had rotted with age so the seamstresses of the town had been hard at work copying the designs and had only just finished in time. In the centre of the platoon, four men carried the Crowning Stone – a simple block with a hollow in the middle. The tower at Migdal had been built to house the Stone in ancient times, and the town had grown around it. The townspeople had done well over the years out of people who had visited as tourists – just to see the tower or to pay a small fortune to look through the tiny barred window into the room where the Stone had been kept all this time. But no one had ever expected to see it used again. Now that it was out in the open, one thing that was widely commented on was its strange colour – almost purple: 'like nothing on earth', was a phrase that people often used to describe it afterwards.

Behind the Stone and its honour guard came an old carved seat – again, found in the tower. It had had to be re-gilded, but now it shone dazzlingly in the sunlight. It was carried at shoulder height on two gilded poles, and supporting these poles should have been the job of the *four* Great Earls. Melech and Zafon took the front ends but at the back, Abaddon had placed two prisoners of war – one from

Earl Jamin's household and the other from Earl Rakath's. The captives had both been dressed in rich robes but at every step there were tell-tale clinks from the shackles round their ankles. Not much was added to the weight of the golden seat by the person sitting on it – high above the procession sat the frail figure of Sir Shamma, the counterfeit messenger, his long white hair braided, wearing a simple robe of white silk.

After this first party, there was a gap of about twenty metres then came Abaddon. He was led by two children, one holding each hand. This, Lord Zemira had explained to him, was to symbolise that he was to be a parent to the Kingdom, and that he was led to the duty by something more than his own will. It was hard to tell from Abaddon's grim face how he was taking this part of the proceedings but Zemira could guess – the cursing that there had been when he had first described it to Abaddon was still fresh in his memory. Lord Zemira himself, as Master of Ceremonies, followed a few paces behind Abaddon, leading half a dozen more children who carried the King's Sword, his robes, and his crown. At this stage Abaddon himself was dressed in a simple linen shirt and purple velvet breeches, and for once in his life, he was unarmed.

Another twenty metres separated Abaddon and his retinue from the remainder of the procession. This was made up of the Town Council of Migdal – who were the ancient Guardians of the Stone and all that went with it – followed by every lord, baron and knight in the Kingdom. At least, that was what Zemira's texts called for – in reality, of course, it was only those nobles who were not currently at war with the King-to-be. Finally, making up the greatest part of the procession, came merchants, yeomen and peasants. These, according to Zemira, were supposed to be representatives sent from every city, town and village of the Kingdom but again, the war ruled out any representation from the south and west. However, Abaddon was pleased to have been informed that some captives fresh from the conquest of the castle at Mesaloth would be in the procession. And last in the ranks of the nobles was another prize that gave Abaddon great pleasure – the solid figure of Baron Medan of Mesaloth, in chains and limping from his wounds.

It took two long hours for the procession to reach the Heights of Ataroth then to climb to the summit, and for all to be arranged in their rightful places according to the ancient formulas. In the centre of the oval plateau at the top of the mound was the Crowning Stone. Three paces away from its corners stood the two Great Earls and the two captive representatives of the rebel Earls; at either side of the Stone stood Sir Shamma and Lord Zemira; in front, but not yet sitting on the Stone, was Abaddon; and in front of *him* were the children with the royal robes and symbols of office. Twenty metres away from this central group began circles of all the remaining members of the procession – first the Guardians of the Stone then the nobles according to their ranks, followed by the common people according to theirs. And at the foot of the mound, standing to attention all along the tops of the three earthen ramparts, were soldiers of Abaddon's Grand Army. Of all the things that caused Abaddon anxiety that day, this was perhaps the most troubling – that his soldiers were so far away. But Zemira had said the texts were clear – no soldier was allowed upon the Heights of Ataroth nor any weapon except the Sword of the King. Even those who had been guarding the captives had had to stay below. The only comfort for Abaddon was that if there was just a single weapon allowed on the

Heights, he was the one who had it.

At last, everything was arranged and at a signal from Lord Zemira, a squad of heralds drawn up in a line behind the Stone blew a fanfare on their clarions. There was silence and complete stillness as Lord Zemira announced that the whole Kingdom would now show its wish that Earl Abaddon should be King by kneeling before him according to their ranks and positions. He signalled again and there was another clarion blast. At this, the two Great Earls knelt. The promise of being burned alive afterwards if they failed to kneel proved as effective as a sword in the back with the two captives and they, too, sank to their knees. Another blast followed and the Guardians knelt, then another and the nobles followed suit. Someone kicked the legs out from under Baron Medan, and thanks to his chains and his wounds, he went down and was unable to rise again.

A final fanfare then it was the turn of the common people of the Kingdom. Once they were all on their knees, the crowning could take place: the 'King Song' would be sung; the children would robe Abaddon; the King's messenger would ask his questions – if he remembered them correctly – then the new King would be crowned. The sound of so many people kneeling at the same time made a dull rumble like a wave running up a pebbled beach. There was a moment's silence and Zemira drew breath to begin his song. But then there was a strange sigh, like the tide ebbing away again. It was the combined gasp of all those who had suddenly noticed that something was wrong. When everyone else had knelt, a small group of commoners in the outer ring, directly opposite to Abaddon, had remained firmly on their feet.

ChAPTER SEVEN

baddon stared hard at the group that was standing defiantly when everyone else on the Heights was kneeling before him. They were too far away for him to see them distinctly, but they all seemed to be wearing hooded cloaks. Then they started moving – carefully and deliberately they picked their way through the kneeling ranks in front of them until they reached the clear ground in the centre of the flat hilltop. Then they marched briskly towards Abaddon in military style – two lines of six, and at their head, a man who was as tall as Abaddon himself. The robber chief looked quickly at Lord Zemira but his Master of Ceremonies was baffled – there was nothing in his ancient books to cover something like this. Then Abaddon measured the distance from himself to the King's Sword held by the children and estimated the point at which he would make a leap for it.

But the point wasn't reached. This mysterious squad, hoods still shadowing their faces, came to a halt before they reached the children. They were near enough to Abaddon for him to see them clearly now, if they chose to reveal themselves, but far enough away to make it necessary to shout anything that had to be said. Whatever happened next would be witnessed by the whole gathering and all the watchers shuffled on their knees and craned their necks to get a better look. Abaddon's eyes flicked repeatedly from the group to the sword and back as seconds passed. These hooded forms seemed inhuman, like something from another world come to take him away. Abaddon felt strength seeping out of him and he began to sweat.

'Who *are* you?' he demanded, at last.

He had meant his voice to be loud and threatening – the kind of voice an adult would use to a trespassing child – but the words came out surprisingly weakly. There was certainly no sign that the strangers were intimidated by them.

In his own time, the leader of the party finally drew back his hood revealing long, dark hair and a gaunt, thin face with piercing eyes.

'My name's Baladan,' he said.

The Heights came alive with sound as people muttered to their neighbours and passed the word back to those who hadn't heard.

'Silence!' Abaddon roared, asserting himself at last, and the crowd was hushed. 'Get off my hill!' he shouted at Baladan.

The rest of the group now revealed their faces. They were Baladan's twelve friends and Abaddon glared at the one among them that he knew. Zethar had clearly failed to honour his secret agreement with Abaddon to feed Baladan to the Great Dragon and Abaddon was not used to people failing to carry out his orders. The punishment for disobedience was death and Zethar felt the threat of murder in the robber's stare. But he held those bulging bull's eyes and didn't look away. Apart from Baladan himself, Zethar was perhaps the only person in the Kingdom who wasn't afraid of Abaddon. Zethar feared nothing but the Great Dragon, the one thing in his life that had ever made him run away.

'*Whose* hill? Baladan replied – and although he didn't shout, his voice seemed to set the air trembling all the way to Migdal.

It didn't look as if Abaddon wanted to argue the point.

'What are you doing here?' he demanded.

'I bring a message from the King of Kings!' Baladan told him.

Again the crowd buzzed but this time it was Baladan who

took control. He raised his hand and the hilltop fell silent.

'The King's messenger is already here,' Lord Zemira butted in, gesturing to Sir Shamma.

Baladan fixed the counterfeit knight with a look that was stern but not unkind.

'Go home to your stories and your dreams, old man,' he said.

And Shamma simply did as he was told. He shuffled off into the kneeling crowd and began picking his way back down the hill. No one tried to stop him.

Now Baladan turned his attention to the crowd.

'On your feet!' he ordered. 'No one is to kneel before this man!'

They obeyed without a word. Abaddon stared round wildly and he knew in his heart that if he commanded them to kneel again, they would not.

'What's your message then, errand boy?' he snarled, with as much contempt as he could muster.

'The message from the King is this,' Baladan announced to the whole gathering. 'The coronation of Abaddon the robber has no authority. It is meaningless. It is not to take place. The King of Kings sends a reminder to this land that it has no king but him. More than a generation ago, your ancestors took the decision, in High Council of the Great Earls and their advisers, that there should be no king here any longer – too many had abused their office and failed their people. It was decided that the Council of Earls should rule under the orders of the King who is King of all lands in creation – the King of Kings himself. The years have caused you to forget your decision made so long ago – you no longer remember there is a King of Kings, let alone seek out his orders. I am here to remind you.'

Baladan waited a moment for this to sink in then turned his attention back to Abaddon.

'And one other thing,' he said. 'Get off *my* hill! Ataroth is no place for a thief.'

This was too much, and with something like his old battle roar, Abaddon lunged for the King's Sword. As he did so, Baladan performed a swirling movement with his cloak, laying bare a huge scabbard hanging down his back; and in the moment that Abaddon snatched the King's Sword from the three children who held it, Baladan unsheathed his own blade. Light exploded across the hilltop as if the sun had dropped amongst them from the sky and all the watchers gasped, covering their faces. Even Abaddon threw his free arm across his eyes and staggered blindly back.

It only lasted an instant then the crowd was able to focus again on the confrontation. Abaddon stood blinking but still holding his sword raised at the ready. The children had scattered when Abaddon had leapt among them and Baladan was now positioned two swords' lengths in front of the robber chief, the point of his weapon resting on the ground.

'Only the King's Sword is allowed on the Heights of Ataroth,' Lord Zemira bleated from behind Abaddon's shoulder.

'Exactly,' said Baladan, not moving and not taking his eyes off Abaddon.

Abaddon fought inside himself to keep control. His great chest was heaving.

'Prove it,' he bellowed. 'Prove you're from the King of Kings. You don't look much like a king's messenger to me!'

He threw his head back and gave a harsh bark that was supposed to be a laugh. But the crowd stayed silent and when he looked around he saw that all attention was riveted on Baladan, waiting for his reply.

'If you want proof, have this,' said Baladan. 'I challenge you. I challenge you to meet the Great Dragon – the source of all dragons. The Champion's crown at the Tournament was meant for the one who would defeat the dragons – you stole that crown. Now see if you can face the consequences of wearing it. You've caused a war and you're hiding behind it – hoping it will make people forget that the real evil in this land is caused by the dragons and that it's your job to destroy them. You haven't even faced *one* dragon since you stole the Champion's crown, yet if you are to do your Champion's duty, you must take on the greatest dragon of them all. Unless the Great Dragon is destroyed, there will never be an end to the plague of dragons in this land. If you face the Great Dragon and defeat it you will have *earned* the authority of the King of Kings to rule the Kingdom because you will have *saved* the Kingdom.'

'Why are you challenging *me*?' Abaddon replied, sourly, 'I asked about you.'

'The same goes for me,' Baladan answered. 'I shall face the Great Dragon – and return. Then you will know who I am.' He threw back his head and proclaimed to the whole crowd: 'The one who defeats the Great Dragon has authority from the King of Kings – pay heed to no one else!'

And even the soldiers on the ramparts below the Heights heard every word.

It was evening and the flickering oil lamps in Abaddon's tent made the robber's bloated face look as if it was peering at Zethar through fire. It had been chaos after Baladan's challenge – the crowd had surged off the Heights of Ataroth, driven wild with excitement and desperate to spread the news of what had happened throughout the land. Baladan himself and his friends had simply melted into the mob and had apparently disappeared as mysteriously as they had come. But not before Abaddon had taken advantage of the confusion and told Zemira and Earl Zafon to seize Zethar. The robber chief, uncrowned, had beaten a retreat to his tent with this one prize and had spent the rest of the afternoon re-establishing order in his army. It was an army that was now significantly reduced – after the disaster on the Heights, Earl Melech had mustered his forces in marching order and was even now on his way eastwards, heading away from Abaddon's camp and back to his own lands. His future intentions were not clear. His parting words had been that Abaddon would never take up Baladan's challenge because he was a fake.

'You see now?' Abaddon growled at Zethar. 'You see now why you must do what I ordered?'

He would have had Zethar cut in pieces for his failure but his captive had assured him that he was still intending to carry out the robber's command. They had been on their way to the Great Dragon, Zethar told him, and it was only news of the coronation that had diverted Baladan. Abaddon cursed himself when he heard this news – the whole coronation project had turned out to be a fiasco in every way.

'How can I build an army to fight this Great Dragon if Baladan can pull a stunt like today?' Abaddon told Zethar. 'Melech's gone with his men – who knows what's next? He can't be left alive – he's too dangerous.'

'You *will* march against the Great Dragon, then?' Zethar asked. 'You *will* take up the challenge?'

It had been Abaddon's failure to accept Baladan's challenge on the Heights that had caused the break-up of the assembly. As he'd stood before Baladan, silent and confused, it had seemed that he had abdicated before he had even been crowned. For the time being, his power was broken and the crowd simply walked away from him.

Zethar had been shocked and had lingered for a moment – just long enough to get himself captured.

'Yes, yes,' Abaddon sighed, 'all in good time.'

Abaddon, sitting at a table in his tent, waved his hand wearily. Zethar, standing on the other side of the table, thought the giant robber looked completely drained. He was slumped in the wooden throne that had been made for him and his eyes slowly closed. Zethar thought Abaddon had fallen asleep and wondered if he should leave. He glanced at the guards on either side of the tent flaps but they were gazing straight ahead without expression. Suddenly Abaddon's eyes jerked open again and he sat up sharply, thumping the table with his huge fist.

'Go!' he shouted at Zethar. 'Feed him to the Dragon – do it now!'

Baladan had given his friends instructions to meet at a certain tavern in Migdal if they should be separated during the coronation. This was where Zethar went after Abaddon let him go. He knew that the friends would all be gathered in a room that Baladan had hired upstairs, but he didn't feel ready to go up straight away. The big drinking room on the ground floor was packed – standing room only – and it took Zethar a long time to get himself served with a pot of strong ale. But when he did, he stayed downstairs in the crowd, picking up snatches of conversation from the excited hubbub in the room. Everyone was shouting to make themselves heard, shoving their red, sweaty faces right up to those they were trying to talk to. It was impossible to follow a whole exchange but it was clear that there was only one subject on people's minds – the events on the Heights of Ataroth, particularly what Baladan's intervention was all about.

'I didn't even think he *existed*!' Zethar heard someone shout.

'How do you know it *was* Baladan?' someone else bawled back.

'Did you *see* that sword?'

'Was *that* the King's Sword?'

'Is *Baladan* the King?'

'He's just a woodsman – he's no more a king than Abaddon!'

'What did Baladan mean, "Get off *my* hill"?'

'He was right about the dragons, though – they're the *real* problem.'

'I had to send six of my best sheep to one last month for a sacrifice.'

'I had to send my son.'

Eventually Zethar, jostled up against a wall, lost his concentration. The talk in the room became blurred into meaningless noise and his mind sank into its own thoughts. Abaddon's failure on the Heights of Ataroth and the way Baladan had stood up to him had thrown Zethar into confusion once again. The thought of Abaddon ruling the Kingdom was sickening – if there was another way of destroying the Great Dragon, Zethar would support it. After the meeting with Jalam, it had seemed clear once again that Baladan was refusing to fight. But on the Heights, Baladan had said quite unmistakably that he would face the Great Dragon. If only he would now show some sign of wanting to take command of the Grand Army and lead it against the monster, Zethar would give him his backing and Abaddon could rot.

Baladan was surrounded by his friends in the upper room and they were all talking to him at once but he still turned to the doorway the moment that Zethar came through it. The two stared at each other for a moment as the babble from the others went on.

'You're back, then,' Baladan said to Zethar.

Many times in the past months Zethar had wondered if Baladan suspected that he was under orders from Abaddon, but that look and those words seemed to say that he knew everything. It suddenly flashed into Zethar's mind that Baladan had made no attempt to rescue him from Abaddon on the Heights – as if he was content to let him be taken.

'Are you all right?' Chilion asked, coming up to his friend. 'Baladan said you had a job to do.'

Zethar said nothing, glad that he didn't have to come up with some other story to cover his absence, and Chilion didn't insist on an answer. The previous year, Zethar had been missing for a long time on a secret mission for Baladan so the friends were used to some mystery surrounding him. Last year, the mission had turned out to be one which involved finding the Great Dragon. Perhaps this time Zethar was involved in organising the army to fight it, Chilion thought. Certainly the possibility of finally taking up arms to do battle with the monster seemed nearer than ever – it had been in everyone's mind since they'd come down from the Heights of Ataroth.

'Did you hear them chanting?' Chilion asked Zethar.

'It was great, wasn't it?' Rizpa said, coming to join them. '"Bal-a-dan!' Bal-a-dan! Dragon Slayer, Bal-a-dan!"'

Rizpa's sister, Lexa, came over now and the three sat at a long table that had been set out with food.

'What I can't understand,' she said, 'is how we got off the Heights without being recognised. I mean, there we were in the middle of a crowd chanting about Baladan and they had Baladan right there in among them but they didn't seem to realise.'

'They're all talking about him downstairs,' Zethar told

them. 'The place is wild for Baladan but no one seems to know he's in a room over their heads.'

The rest came to the table and they started to eat. It was good food and there was plenty of it – plenty of wine too. After all their months of rough living on the road and the triumph of the day, the gathering had the atmosphere of a victory party.

'I haven't felt this good since The Dragon of Kiriath was killed!' Zilla shouted, raising a wineskin and squirting it over her face.

There was a lot of laughter – everyone was in high spirits. Everyone except Zethar and Baladan. Baladan seemed detached and thoughtful although he smiled at everything that was said to him; and Zethar was tense and preoccupied. The two exchanged looks several times – Zethar searching their leader's face for some sign but without success; and Baladan with a strange, sad expression that made Zethar feel almost as if he was being pitied. Each time, that look made him go hot inside and he turned away.

'When we've got our army,' Ruel announced to the table, waving a chicken leg like a weapon, 'and we've smashed Abaddon and we've hacked the Great Dragon into a million bits and Baladan's crowned King, I'm going to be his Grand General! What about you, Zilla?'

'Oh, me, dearie? – I'll be the royal storyteller and keeper of the records,' she said. 'And I think Zabad should be in charge of all the money.'

Zabad pulled a face and waved his hand.

'I want to be the top judge,' Rizpa shouted, and she started pointing at them one by one, saying, 'Off with his head!'

Soon everyone was having a go.

'I'm going to be in charge of all the castles,' Chilion boasted. 'What do you want to do, Zethar?'

But Zethar wasn't playing. He stared hard at Baladan and the table fell silent.

'*Are* you going to take on Abaddon now?' he asked. '*Are* you going to take his forces from him and lead the Grand Army like the Champion was supposed to do? *Are* you going to lead us against the Great Dragon?'

Baladan made them wait a long moment. The only sound was the crackling of the logs in the big fireplace and the hubbub from the drinking hall downstairs. Baladan looked slowly at each one of them in turn then settled his gaze on Zethar.

'No,' he replied, quietly. 'No, I'm not.'

There was another moment for this to sink in then everyone was talking at once. The confrontation with Abaddon had seemed such a turning point that none of them had doubted that things would change from now on. But here was Baladan with the same old refusal to do the one thing that everyone knew he *had* to do for anything to make sense. All the old arguments came out again in a jumble of sound until Baladan put his hand up for silence.

'I've told you many times,' he said, 'no army in the Kingdom can stand against the Great Dragon. They'd all be killed – a senseless waste. Nothing's changed about that. What's happened today doesn't alter that in the slightest.'

Zethar's gaze dropped and he stared at the remains of the food on the wooden board in front of him.

'Nevertheless, the time to meet the Great Dragon *has* come,' Baladan went on.

'But how,' Thassi asked, 'if we don't have an army?'

'Only *I* can meet this dragon,' Baladan answered. 'Zethar will show me the way but I must meet it alone.'

'Then you'll die,' Chilion told him flatly. 'You'll die and it'll all be over – what's the *point*? Don't you care about us? Don't you care about *anything*?'

It was Baladan's turn to stare at the table now.

'You're right,' he said, quietly. 'It will be an ending – a *kind* of ending. But endings can also be beginnings.'

The party was clearly over and Baladan led his friends out into the moonlit streets of Migdal. Despondent – even betrayed – though they were feeling, none of them refused to come with Baladan when he wrapped his hooded cloak around him and asked them to keep him company. After all this time, they felt bound to this strange man. No one knew what kind of a beginning could be in store but every one sensed that an ending was certainly in sight and they all knew that they would have to see things through. The only one who might have refused to come was Zethar but his decision had been made for him by Baladan's response. Sickening though it was, his only hope was now with Abaddon. Zethar knew he must lead Baladan to the Great Dragon and his death and to do that, he too would have to stay with their leader to the end.

Migdal was still a place of excitement as the group of thirteen cloaked figures slipped through its narrow streets. Singing and shouting could be heard from the taverns. Some of the musicians who had come to play at the celebrations after the coronation had decided they might as well play anyway, and were out in the square with a crowd around them. Everyone had intended to have a party once the new king was crowned and now there almost seemed *more* to celebrate – Abaddon looked as if he'd been bested; the legendary Baladan had appeared in their midst like something out of a fairy tale with the promise of a show-down with the Great Dragon; and they'd been told that if the Great Dragon was destroyed, the Old Kingdom could be set free at last from its plague of monsters.

But Baladan wasn't taking his friends on a tour of the celebrations in Migdal. Instead, he led them straight out of the town towards the Heights of Ataroth, a smooth black outline against the deep blue of the night sky. They were aware that Abaddon's camp lay in their path but they could neither see nor hear any sign of it. It seemed as if Abaddon must have ordered 'lights out' because everything ahead was darkness and silence. Baladan led them in a wide arc as if he knew exactly where the camp was, then on until they reached the first of the earth ramparts that surrounded the Heights. They climbed in silence, all of them wondering why Baladan wanted them out here in the night but none of them willing to ask. At last they reached the summit and Baladan stopped at the edge of the oval plateau, looking back across the plain below.

They'd been too preoccupied earlier to spend time admiring the view but now that the day and its events were over, they all stood quietly and gazed around them. It was a cloudless night and the moon was bright enough for them to see the landscape laid out for miles in a surprising variety of dark blues and greys. Here and there, the moonlight turned stretches of water into ribbons or patches of bright silver. It was obvious that this ancient site had been chosen because it gave a view over a vast area. The plain on which it had been raised was already high and the narrow passes that led to it must have provided a good defence centuries before Jalam had used them to try and hold off Abaddon's advance.

Baladan looked around him at the lands of the Old Kingdom for a long time, then he tilted his head back and stared at the stars above in their thousands. Ruel watched him closely, all the time trying to hold in his mind an image of the knight in golden armour that Baladan had become as they'd looked down the radiant valley to the castle of the

King of Kings. There seemed no connection between that shining, magnificent figure and the sad looking man who stood here gazing at the stars. Ruel couldn't help asking himself if the incident at the mysterious valley had all been some strange waking dream – the valley and the golden armour *had* disappeared, after all. Everything had seemed possible after they'd seen the castle of the King; and Baladan had seemed to be moving in the right direction at last – the one they all wanted him to take. But now they seemed to be back where they'd started again, with nothing to look forward to but Baladan's senseless death.

'Come with me,' Baladan said, softly, and walked away across the oval.

The twelve friends followed and made a ragged semi-circle round him when he stopped again. He was looking at a large rectangle of crushed grass. It was the place where the Crowning Stone had been placed. The Stone and everything else to do with the coronation had been cleared hours ago. The plateau was completely empty now, apart from the figures of Baladan and his friends, like insects on the giant bulk of the Heights of Ataroth.

'Stay awake with me,' Baladan said, and he sat down in the space where the Stone had been, with his knees up to his chin and his wrists resting on them. It was the way Ruel remembered him sitting the first time they'd met – by a campfire in the forest of Kiriath when Ruel had set off on his quest to find the King. Ruel and the others sat down on the grass around their friend and waited to see what would happen next.

Baladan stayed absolutely still, at rest but alert, and slowly the minutes built up until they had been there for nearly an hour. One by one, the friends curled up on the ground and made themselves as comfortable as they could, wrapped in their thick cloaks. They were used to sleeping out of doors, and by the time they had been there for an hour and a half, every one of them was asleep – every one except Ruel. His eyelids were heavy and his head kept sinking then jerking up again, but he was determined to stay awake – it was what Baladan had asked. He felt he owed it to a friend. When it came down to it what caused Ruel more distress than anything – even more than losing the hope that the King's valley and the confrontation with Abaddon had given him – was that thought that he was going to lose his friend.

Ruel's mind began to work on the problem. Maybe they could prevent Baladan meeting the Great Dragon. Maybe they could talk him out of it. They'd never talked him out of anything in all the time they'd known him but it was still worth a try. In the morning, he'd have a go at it. Or maybe he could get Zethar to say he'd forgotten where the Great Dragon lived or get him to take Baladan to the wrong place and pretend the monster had simply given up and left. He imagined how the conversation would go. He pictured the place they would take Baladan – somewhere by the sea. They'd point over the waves and say that the Great Dragon had flown away. As he visualised the scene, Ruel could feel the heat of the sun and hear the gentle swish of the waves.

His head jerked up and he realised he must have been asleep for quite some time. Slowly he pieced together where he was and what was going on and looked at Baladan. His friend no longer seemed relaxed – he was kneeling now and his back was rigid. His hands were clasped tight in front of him and his head was thrown back, but he wasn't looking at the stars – his eyes were tight shut. His whole body was shaking, like a man with a fever.

'What is it?' Ruel whispered.

Baladan didn't open his eyes or show any sign that he'd heard. Nor did he turn to Ruel when he replied a moment later.

'I'm going to die,' he said. 'All I can see is the ending.'

It may have been a trick of the moonlight but Baladan's face seemed to be wet with sweat, or tears. He didn't speak again. Ruel fought to keep his eyes open and watch over his friend, but a few minutes later his head sank onto his chest once more, and all thoughts were lost in the blankness of exhausted sleep.

chapter eight

*A*pril began with simmering sunshine. Even in the shade of the forest the air was warm and alive with the song of birds and the lazy hum of insects. But where Nara and the rest of the war orphans were gathered, the hum had turned into a maddening buzz that drowned the birdsong and every other sound. It was so loud you could hardly think. The other children were swiping wildly at the air round their heads but Nara stood still, her attention focused on the cause of the disturbance. Twenty metres in front of them, surrounded by a dense cloud of feasting flies, were half a dozen dead bodies. By the nauseating smell, they'd been there some time.

This was not the first pile of bodies the gang had found. It was nearly two months now since the city of Mesaloth had fallen, and in that time, General Oreb's men had been working their way through the forest killing anyone they met, no matter who they were or who they supported. Three weeks ago, the castle itself had finally been taken and since then, the situation had become much worse. All Oreb's men were now free to sweep the forest, and the war orphans had been pushed steadily further and further south as the general's army moved on towards Earl Jamin's fortress and final victory.

'Come on, Nara!' Penina shouted above the brain-jamming whine of the flies. 'What's the point of hanging around?'

But Nara stayed where she was, just wafting her hand from time to time to keep the insects from settling on her face.

'I'm thinking,' she said.

It was Nara's coolness and her ability to think things through that had impressed the gang of war orphans most after they had lost their leader, Aia, seven weeks ago. Once her ankle had healed, Nara had shown herself to be as strong and daring as any of them. But it was her cunning that had proved the most useful, saving them from disaster several times – and it was this that had eventually made her their undisputed leader. Now they waited patiently for her latest thoughts.

'We'll have to leave the forest,' she said at last, turning away from the rotting pile.

'But how will we live?' Penina asked, panic-stricken. 'We don't know how to live anywhere else.'

'Soon there'll be nothing left to live *on,*' Nara replied. 'The more people Oreb's men kill, the fewer there are for us to steal from.'

It was true and they all knew it. They lived by stealing, far more than by hunting – any group of survivors hiding in the forest was fair game for them and they cared as little as Oreb's men themselves which side their victims were on.

'Soon we'll be the only ones left in the forest and Oreb will drive us out like the rest,' Nara went on. 'It's time to go before we're pushed – or end up as food for flies.'

Late that afternoon, Nara and her gang lay hidden amongst the last trees on the southern fringe of the forest. They could see smoke rising from a small collection of cottages about half a kilometre away.

'That's how we'll live,' Nara told them. 'There must be hundreds of villages like that to rob.'

'But how?' one of them asked, desperately.

Nara unslung her bow. It was her prize possession, taken from a soldier they'd ambushed and killed. She'd learned to shoot it like a marksman and it had played a key role in many of their exploits but now she passed it, with her quiver, to one of the oldest of her gang.

'Look after it,' she ordered. 'Stay here, all of you – I only need Penina for this.'

＊＊＊

Nara and Penina were quite close to the ring of cottages that marked the boundary of the settlement before they saw their first villager – a man, chopping wood. He was making such a noise and concentrating so hard that he didn't notice the pair until they were nearly up to him but then they made sure he knew they were there.

'Help!' Penina shouted. 'Please help us!'

Nara was gripping Penina's hand, and limping, the way she had when they'd first met. The man looked round just in time to take this in before Nara rolled up her eyes and collapsed in a heap. Penina started shaking her and babbling hysterically.

'Wake up! Wake up! Nara!' she cried. 'We've made it. We're safe. Don't give up now. These people will look after us. We're safe at last.'

'Don't worry, little girl,' the man said, as he bent over Nara's crumpled body. 'She's still breathing. She'll live. Don't cry.'

Penina was a natural actor and had managed to make herself blubber by now.

'It's all right,' the man went on. 'Don't worry. We'll look after you.'

'Oh, thank you, thank you!' Penina burst out, grabbing the man round his legs and wiping her wet cheeks on his breeches.

'Come on, then,' said the man, laughing. 'Let me go and we'll get your friend into my cottage – it's just here. My wife will see to her.'

He was a strong man, and when Penina released his legs, he scooped Nara into his arms and carried her through the doorway of the nearest cottage.

'Here's a strange find for you, mother,' he called to his wife, as he stepped over the threshold.

Like all poor people's cottages in the Old Kingdom, this was a gloomy little place, lit only by a tiny unglazed hole for a window, light from the doorway and the open fire burning in the middle of the single room.

'Who is it?' squeaked a little voice. A boy of about three appeared from the shadows to inspect their guests as the man's wife turned from the corner where she was working.

'Now *that* I don't know, ' the man said, laying Nara on his bed – a pile of straw by the wall. 'But one thing I *do* know is that she needs some food – they both look starving. Is that right, little one?' he asked Penina.

'Oh, *yes!*' Penina told him. 'We haven't eaten for – I can't remember how long.'

The woman straightened up, rubbing the aching small of her back, and looked the pair over critically.

'Well, we've little enough to eat ourselves,' she said, 'thanks to the Great Dragon.'

'Dragon?' Penina said, genuinely alarmed.

'Don't worry, little one,' the man said. 'It won't bother us again in Helez for a while. As long as we leave food in the forest for it, it stays away from our village. We've just taken it some this week.'

'*Some?*' his wife exploded. 'We've given it nearly *everything* – and harvest's *months* away. We've nothing left for ourselves, never mind strangers.'

'Oh, we've a little put by, surely, mother,' the man said. 'Look at the state of these little ones!'

'That one's not so little,' the woman said sharply, pointing at Nara. But still, she went to a corner of the room and started searching out something to eat. At once, Nara opened her eyes a fraction and watched closely through her lashes.

'The forest?' Penina said, in a shaky voice. 'Did you say this Great Dragon lives in the *forest*?'

Penina and the rest of the gang came from villages to the north of Mesaloth. They, too, had been stripped for years of their food and many of their people by a dragon that plagued their region – but it lived in a cave at the top of a mountain. Penina and the others had never considered that dragons could live where *people* might go; and to avoid a paralysing panic, Nara had kept Mesaloth's legends about the Great Dragon's lair to herself.

'Dragon in forest,' the little boy said, coming up and touching Penina's hand.

'But *we've* been in the forest,' she said. 'We've been in there for ages!'

Penina sat down heavily next to Nara, apparently unconscious, and held on to her hand.

'Where have you come from?' the woman asked.

'Mesaloth,' Penina told her.

'And you didn't know where the Great Dragon lives?' she asked, with a hint of suspicion in her voice.

'You'll be for Baladan, then,' the man said.

Penina didn't answer until Nara gripped her hand hard then she remembered the instructions Nara had given her as they'd walked from the forest to this village of Helez.

'Who are *you* for?' Penina asked.

'Baladan, of course,' the man said. 'He's the only one that can get rid of dragons and that's what we need if we're going to put this Kingdom right.'

'Yes, *we're* for Baladan too,' Penina told him.

'Baladan!' the little boy piped up, and the man ruffled his hair proudly.

'That's right, soldier,' he said. 'What were people saying about Baladan in Mesaloth?' he asked Penina. 'People in these parts have been saying that he's really a Champion sent from the King himself. There's even a rumour that he might be the King's son, though I don't see how that could be.'

At this point, Nara decided her young accomplice was probably getting out of her depth so she gave a groan, opened her eyes and started struggling to sit up. That was the signal for their meagre portion of food to be served and talk moved to other things. Nara acted out the part of someone slowly reviving and gradually she unfolded a long story about the adventures she and Penina had had in their trek through the forest after Mesaloth's fall. Some of it was based on the truth but many parts were made up – such as Nara's claim that she and Penina were sisters. Penina particularly liked that part. In fact, she was enjoying the whole business.

After their scrap of food, rest was prescribed for the visitors. It was dark now and anyway, no one stayed up long once the last light had gone so the family rearranged their straw to make an extra bed for their guests and settled down for the night.

Nara and Penina pretended to go to sleep straight away but they were really wide awake and heard perfectly as the man whispered, 'Couldn't they stay with us?'

They also heard his wife's reply: 'They could *not*. We're starving already.'

They said nothing more and when gentle snoring had been coming from the couple for a few minutes, the visitors slowly got up from their straw mattress. The embers of the fire gave off a dull red glow – just enough light for Nara to find her way to the place where she'd seen the woman get the extra supplies. The woman hadn't lied – there really was very little to spare: two large brown loaves, a canvas bag that seemed to be full of oatcakes, half a cheese and some vegetables that felt like turnips. Nara took as much as the two of them could store in their clothes. Then they turned to the door, ready to go – and stopped dead.

Standing by the glowing embers, gazing at them with wide eyes, was the little boy.

'You want more?' he asked, brightly.

Nara put her fingers to her lips and shushed but the boy turned to where his parents were sleeping and called out loud and clear, 'Mummy! Daddy! They want more!'

His parents were awake at once and in an instant, the man realised what was going on: his visitors were standing right by the family store and their clothes were bulging. He drew breath to speak, but the words never came out. Nara's sharp eyes had already seen, earlier in the evening, that a knife was kept close to the food store. The room was so small that she was able to reach out for the knife with one hand and lunge for the boy with the other before the man could react. By the time he was on his feet, Nara had his son firmly in her grasp, the knife pressed to his neck.

'Come near us and he's dead,' she told them.

The man and his wife froze. Nara and Penina edged towards the door. Nara hoisted the petrified boy off the ground to carry him away and it was only then that he came to life, kicking and screaming. But Nara had him in a powerful grip with the knife still at his throat and quickly the two raiders got out of the cottage door. The parents followed but Nara turned on them.

'Stay there,' she ordered. 'If you stay where you are, I'll let him go as soon we're clear.'

The boy's screams had woken the rest of Helez and Nara could see the shadows of other people coming out of their cottages.

'That goes for the rest of you,' she shouted. 'Come after us and we'll kill him.'

Then she and Penina turned and ran as fast as the struggling child and stolen food would let them.

The night was cloudy and it was impossible to make out much but Nara guessed they must be about halfway back to the tree line. She was beginning to think about letting the child go when suddenly the survival senses she'd developed in the forest told her something was ahead.

At the same moment a deep voice shouted out, 'Stop where you are!'

Nara could just see the shape of a man about ten metres ahead.

They had left confusion in Helez. Not everyone realised the details but it didn't take long for the word to go round that a couple of children had run off with food from the village and some of the men had immediately gone after the thieves before the frantic parents could explain about the kidnap and stop them. One of these pursuers had managed to outstrip the raiders and he was barring their way.

'If you come near us, I'll kill the boy,' Nara snarled and she raised the knife in the hope that the man would see and think she meant business.

But it was Penina who saw Nara's arm move and it was too much for her. She thought the boy really *was* going to be stabbed.

'No!' she yelled, and grabbed her friend's arm.

In the brief struggle, the boy wriggled free and the man threw himself towards the kidnappers. He got to Nara just as she managed to push Penina away from her.

'Run, Penina!' Nara called into the darkness, as the man crashed into her and wrestled her to the ground.

She sank the knife into him twice before he finally

clamped her wrist, and by then, three more men had arrived.

Nara kicked, bit and lashed out all the way back to Helez, but it was no good. Her weapon was gone, and arms like iron were holding her. She was caught.

When Nara was led out for trial next morning, her wrists and ankles were raw from the rope that had been bound round them and her body was aching from the discomfort of lying tied up all night on the hard earth of a cattle pen but to her surprise, she felt a strange sense of relief. First she was relieved that she was the only one being led out to the open ground where the trial was to take place – that meant Penina had got away; but more than that, she realised she felt relieved that, for her, everything was finally over.

She looked towards the distant line of trees and knew that her gang would already be on their way out of this danger area, considering who should be their next leader. There would be no rescue attempt – even little Penina wouldn't suggest it. And just as she expected nothing from the gang, Nara expected nothing from her trial – the villagers would kill her, without a doubt. The months of struggle since the first attack on Mesaloth had been so hard and now she couldn't even think what the point of it all had been – apart from simply to stay alive. The survival instinct was as strong in her as ever – she knew that if she could escape now, she would run – but really there seemed nothing to live *for* any more. Her parents and family were dead; her city was destroyed; the whole Kingdom was just a chaotic nightmare. And even if the war ended, the Great Dragon that had drained the riches of Mesaloth for as long as anyone could remember was still on the loose and the whole Kingdom was still infested with dragons. What kind of a place was that to live? She found that deep inside her she was glad she'd finally come to a dead end, that there was no way out and that she didn't have to fight any more.

The place for the trial was in the centre of Helez where its two tracks crossed. Everyone in the village was gathered at this meeting place and there was a lot of hissing and spitting as Nara was dragged between two strong men armed with staves to stand before the village Elder. He was a shrivelled-looking man with a bent back and a long head that nodded uncontrollably; but his eyes were every bit as sharp and hard as Nara's own. To the left of the Elder stood the couple who had been robbed. They had their little boy with them but his face was buried in his mother's skirts and he still seemed to be terrified. On the Elder's right, a man was supporting himself by leaning heavily on a quarterstaff. His left arm was in a sling, and his left thigh was heavily bandaged. He glowered fiercely at Nara.

'What's your name, girl?' the Elder demanded.

'Nara,' she said, with her head held high, refusing to lower her eyes under his glare.

It was all that she *did* say throughout the whole of the short trial. The Elder put the charges to her – theft, kidnap and assault – and asked if she accepted her guilt but she kept silent. The evidence was presented – the stolen goods that had been found on her; the knife that had been taken from her; the wounds of the man leaning on his staff; and the words of such witnesses as there had been. Then the Elder asked if she had anything to say in her defence or to explain her actions and again, she said nothing. The village council, gathered behind the Elder, took only moments to confer and to bring in a verdict of guilty. All that remained was for the Elder to pass sentence. He asked Nara once again if she had anything to say and when she refused to answer, the Elder invited anyone else present to speak before sentence was passed.

Then something happened that finally had some effect on Nara. The man whose cottage she'd robbed and whose child she'd threatened to kill stepped forward. His wife was staring angrily at him and it seemed to take him a while to screw up his courage. But at last he spoke.

'I just have this to say,' he told the gathering, 'she did what she did for a reason. She's only a child – the other one was even younger. Children don't act like this for nothing. I've got a boy – we've all got children – and we know this isn't a natural way for a child to act. She's come from Mesaloth. Think what she must have been through – what she must have seen...'

'How do we *know* where she's come from?' the man's wife interrupted. 'A thief can be a liar, too!' and she turned away from her husband, lifting her child and holding him close against her.

'I don't believe she would have killed our child, I really don't,' the man went on.

Nara looked at him and their eyes met for a moment. She wondered if he was right. She honestly didn't know but she found herself hoping he was.

'She must be punished. Of *course* she must be punished. I *want* her to be punished for the harm she's done us,' the man finished off. 'All that I'm asking is that you be merciful in your sentence.'

The Elder waited for any more comments and when there were none, he fixed Nara with his hard grey eyes.

'The punishment for theft is death,' he told her. 'If you truly are from Mesaloth, then you are a stranger and will not know our ways. The execution of criminals in Helez and every village hereabouts is the work of the Great Dragon. All criminals under sentence of death are left as sacrifices at the monster's lair. However, in view of the plea for mercy we have heard, I will make this qualification in your case: you are to be left for the Great Dragon in the usual way but those who bind you will return in three days. If you have not been devoured, then you will be spared.'

Later that morning, Nara set out on what seemed certain to be her last journey. Helez was too poor a place to afford chains but her arms were well bound behind her back, and a length of rope about half a metre long was tied at each end to her ankles so that she couldn't run. Nara never wasted energy and she knew it was pointless to struggle as she was led towards the forest by two tough-looking villagers. One of them – a square, red-faced man with a neck like a bull – was carrying the stake she would be tied to when they reached the Great Dragon's lair.

'Isn't there a post there already,' Nara asked, 'from the other people you've taken?'

'What do you think the Great Dragon *is*?' said the man with the stake. 'Just some kind of big wolf that'll chew you up in tidy bits?'

'That's a good one, Macca!' the other man said, and they both laughed.

Macca came close to her side. 'It'll take you in one bite,' he whispered, menacingly; then he slapped the sturdy stake he had over his shoulder. 'There won't be anything left of this but a few charred splinters,' he told her.

Macca seemed rather proud of the Great Dragon and as they marched, he started to tell her all about the fearful creature that had menaced the area for generations. For more years than anyone knew, it had demanded a huge share of all that the local villages produced – not to mention periodic human sacrifices which had to be supplied from among the innocent if there were no criminals to execute.

'So we're very glad you came along,' Macca explained, with a nasty grin. 'It means none of us will have to be gobbled up for a while – what do you say, Nabal?'

Nabal agreed and laughed with Macca again.

None of this was news to Nara, as the dragon they were describing was the same one that devoured the wealth and the people of Mesaloth, too. It was just that their sacrifices had to be left by some blackened rocks on the riverbank, a kilometre east of the city and not in the forest. However, what came next *was* information that she'd never heard in Mesaloth.

'Our dragon was the first in all the land,' Macca told her. 'Isn't that right, Nabal?'

Nabal murmured his agreement, not sounding quite so enthusiastic as his companion. He was a tall, athletic man who looked as if he didn't have much reason to be afraid of anyone but he was still darting anxious glances all around him. They were among the trees now and he was obviously starting to feel apprehensive.

'It's the one that every other dragon came from,' Macca went on. 'Once every age, or so they say, it lays an egg. And when that egg hatches, you've got another dragon.'

He came close to her again, thrusting his face towards hers and making her stomach heave with his stinking breath.

'But here's the thing,' he told her. 'The story goes that none of these other dragons can lay eggs – only our Great Dragon. So that's the one old Baladan's got to kill if he wants to get anywhere. Kill the Great Dragon and the whole lot of them are done for! The others can be picked off, one by one, and there won't be any more to replace them.'

At that moment, Nabal grabbed Macca's shoulder and

hissed at him to be quiet. They stood still and listened. Then they heard the sound of people moving through the forest, not far ahead. They were making no attempt to move quietly and there were plenty of them.

'Abaddon's?' Nabal whispered.

'Bound to be,' Macca replied. 'No one else would travel so boldly.'

Immediately Nara's instinct for survival kicked in – whatever side these people were on, they would be a diversion and any chaos she could create might enable her to escape.

'Hey!' she yelled. 'Over here!'

But she didn't manage any more before a huge hand smothered her mouth. She bit hard into the flesh beneath the thumb and Macca pulled his hand away with a yelp but as she drew breath to shout again, a fist slammed into her face and that was that.

When she came round, she found that a gag had been tied tightly across her mouth and the two men were pinning her to the ground. She could hardly breathe, let alone move. They were under some kind of cover and Nara guessed it was a hide that the villagers used for hunting. It was a very good one, too, because it was keeping them hidden even though the people they'd heard coming through the forest were standing all around them. Nara could see their legs and hear their voices.

'It definitely came from near here,' someone was saying.

'They can't just have disappeared,' another voice put in.

'Maybe it was a bird,' someone else said.

'Don't be stupid – it was someone calling, and it came from over here,' the first person insisted.

'We haven't time for this,' another man pointed out. 'The general's orders were to destroy the village and report back before nightfall. We need to move on.'

There were murmurs of agreement, and the patrol began to march away. Nara guessed there must have been about thirty men and by the clanking they were making, they were well armed. There could be no doubt now whose side they were on and no doubt that the village they'd been detailed to destroy was Helez – the first village south of the forest, and firm in its support of Baladan.

'We'll have to warn them,' said Nabal.

'We've got to see to *her*,' Macca reminded him.

'What does *that* matter now?' Nabal asked.

'I'll tell you what,' Macca suggested, 'I'll see to the girl, and you head back to the village. If you run, you'll easily beat that bunch of clodhoppers.'

It was agreed and Nabal set off at speed. It occurred to Nara that Macca had probably got the best deal. She was certain that Oreb's ruthless soldiers would kill everyone in Helez even if they *did* get a warning, which meant that the only villager left alive would be the one leading her to the Great Dragon. She took a sideways look at Macca's face and saw a distinct look of satisfaction on it that suggested she wasn't the only one to have worked out the odds of survival.

Nara knew they had been heading east for most of their journey – into an area of the forest she and her gang had never explored – and when Macca finally stopped, she calculated they had been walking long enough for it to be afternoon.

'Here we are, then,' Macca said cheerfully.

He said it as if they'd arrived at some magnificent palace. Nara could see the trees were thinning out ahead and when Macca led her forward the last few metres, she quickly found herself on the edge of a huge circular clearing, about a quarter of a kilometre across. It was empty but in the middle, there was an area of black, burned earth. It was scattered with bones.

'They say the Great Dragon's as old as the world,' Macca told her, breathing his horrible breath into her face again. 'It's never stopped growing and it's got too big to live in a cave so it has to live here, out in the open. It's as big as a hill and covered with lichen like weathered rock. You're lucky it's not here now, otherwise it'd have you before I could get your stake in the ground. As it is, it might not be back for days.'

He worked the sharp end of the stake into the ground at the edge of the clearing then unslung the heavy hammer that was hanging from his belt.

'If he doesn't come back for *three* days – you're in the clear,' he went on, and started driving the stake in with great, thumping blows.

'That is,' he said, when he'd finished, 'if there's anyone left to come and get you!'

He bound Nara firmly to the stake round her waist and ankles then retied her wrists behind the post and took off her gag.

'You can yell as much as you like now,' he said, 'for all the good it'll do you. No one in their right mind would come near this place.'

All the time they had been marching, Nara had been fighting one last battle – the battle to drive away the thought of her death. She had been determined not to let Macca see her crumble beneath the horror of it. But now, faced with this arena of destruction, she could hold it back no longer. Throughout her short life, as long as there'd been a chance to fight or run, fear had never had power to overcome her; but now, tied up and helpless in the face of death, every muscle in her body began to tremble and nausea flooded her. Her last desperate wish was that Macca would go before she was sick, or worse. He went behind her and she felt the tugging as he checked the knots he'd made

– then nothing: just silence, stillness and the pounding of blood in her head. The silence lengthened until at last she knew she was alone.

ChAPTER NINE

uel, too, was in the forest of Mesaloth. He was sitting on a moss-covered rock in a dismal little clearing, far in among the trees. The rock was beside a dark pool of water and Ruel was staring vacantly into its depths. He couldn't see the bottom at all – just deep, liquid blackness. Everything was gloomy in the clearing – even Baladan's battle sword, lying in its scabbard beside the rock, seemed to have lost its shine in the place. There was no bird song and the only sound was Hesed drinking steadily from the pool. Baladan's weapon and horse were there but not Baladan himself. It was a week since Ruel had last seen his friend and been given charge of Hesed and the great sword. As he gazed into the dark waters, Ruel remembered that meeting – a meeting he was now sure had been final. It had happened on the northern edge of the forest just west of Mesaloth, a week after Abaddon's failed coronation.

The morning after they'd slept out on the Heights of Ataroth, Ruel and his friends had woken to find Baladan gone. Zethar had gone, too, and it was obvious what had happened – Zethar was leading Baladan to the Great Dragon. Baladan had already made it clear that was what he wanted – he'd also made it clear he wanted to meet the monster alone – so the friends who were left on the Heights had decided there was only one thing left for them to do.

'We'll have to find Jalam and join his war band,' Chilion had said.

It was hard to think of simply abandoning Baladan but in the end, everyone had agreed so they'd all slipped back into Migdal, collected their horses from the tavern stable and ridden away south in search of the young warrior.

No one had spoken any more about Baladan but Ruel had been unable to put their leader out of his mind. Time and again, as they rode, he'd wondered where the Great Dragon was hidden. And the more he'd thought about it, the more convinced he'd become – from things Zethar had let slip over the months – that the forest at Mesaloth held vital clues. So early one morning, a couple of days after they'd left the Heights of Ataroth, Ruel had woken Zilla and told her quietly that he was going to search for Baladan. Maybe there was still a way of stopping him going to a pointless death. Zilla was more concerned with stopping Ruel but her pleas were useless and by the time the rest of them were stirring, Ruel was far away.

Five days later, Ruel had reached Mesaloth. He'd forded the river west of the city and there to greet him on the other side had been Baladan. He hadn't seemed at all surprised to see his young friend.

'I've been waiting for you,' he said, and he led him into the cover of the forest fringe.

When they were safely out of sight of Oreb's garrison, guarding the walls of Mesaloth, Baladan called Hesed's name and his warhorse emerged from the shadow of the trees.

Remembering this, as he sat on his mossy rock, Ruel watched Hesed drinking from the dark pool and pictured the way Baladan had stroked his horse's neck, and whispered into his ear. What had happened next still shocked Ruel when he thought of it. Baladan carefully undid the great battle sword in its scabbard from Hesed's saddle, passed Hesed's reins to Ruel and gently hung the sword over his young friend's shoulder.

'I won't be needing these any more. But you will.' Baladan told him. 'Look after Hesed. Use the sword well.'

And with that, he'd turned to walk away.

It was only then that Ruel had realised Baladan was alone.

'Wait!' he called. 'Where's Zethar?'

Baladan paused and turned back for a moment.

'Zethar has done his job,' he explained. 'He's given me all the directions I need but now I must finish the journey alone. Zethar's gone on his way now – and so must you.'

He'd seemed anxious to be off once he'd done his business with Hesed and the sword, and he gave Ruel no opportunity to try and divert him from his mission. He stepped into the shadows and a moment later, he'd disappeared.

Ruel had stood still for a long time, lost in thought, until finally he became aware of the weight of the sword hanging from his shoulder and registered that it wasn't dragging on the ground behind him. It made him realise how much he must have grown in the time he'd known Baladan and it started him thinking over all the things they'd been through together and the times he'd seen Baladan wield the mighty sword that now hung at his back. It was too much – he couldn't just let his friend disappear from his life.

'Even if all the rest give up on you,' he'd said to himself, 'I'm not going to let you go.'

And with that, he'd tied his own horse to Hesed and led them both off in pursuit of Baladan.

What followed was a week of wandering that had brought Ruel at last to the gloomy clearing and the rock by the pool where he now sat with Hesed and the sword. Although Baladan had only had a few minutes' start, Ruel had been unable to find him either then or in subsequent days. But he *had* found plenty of other people in the forest. The place was swarming with Oreb's patrols and Ruel had exhausted most of his energy in avoiding them. Hiding himself was hard enough but the horses had been a nightmare. He had very soon let his own horse go but whenever he thought of leaving Hesed, Baladan's words came into his mind. However, his friend's warhorse was well trained in the art of disappearing and Ruel had soon realised it would be easier if he let Hesed attend to his own safety. After all, Hesed had learned from a master: Baladan seemed able to disappear in the blink of an eye, even in the open. Here in the forest, no one stood a chance of finding him – and that meant, Ruel soon had to recognise, that neither did he. It became clear that the pursuit of Baladan was hopeless and Ruel's spirits gradually ebbed. Now, after a week of fruitless searching, he was hungry, frightened, totally lost – and deep down he had to admit that all he wanted was to get out of the forest alive.

Ruel had been staring miserably into the dark pool for a long time when he was suddenly disturbed by the sound of something crashing through the trees. His first thought was of Oreb's soldiers and he instantly scanned the place for the best spot to hide; but almost immediately his forest upbringing told him the noise was too light for a group of men so he jumped up, slung the great sword over his shoulder in readiness and stood his ground. A moment later, the undergrowth parted and a small boy came stumbling into the clearing, his face scratched, bleeding and wet with tears.

The boy seemed very young to Ruel – no more than three years old – and the two of them stared at each other for a moment. Then the child waved his arms, pointing back in the direction he'd come from.

'Quick!' he piped. 'Come quick!'

'Where?' Ruel asked.

'Village,' the boy said.

Ruel's mind raced. If the boy was as young as he looked, he couldn't have come far on his own, and if he'd come from a village, that meant they must be near the edge of the forest. He felt a sudden surge of hope.

'Show me?' he said, moving towards the boy.

'Use that,' the boy said, pointing at the sword hilt visible over Ruel's shoulder.

'What?'

'Kill people.'

'Why?' Ruel asked.

'Men come – lots and lots – all fighting. You've got to help.'

At once, the probable truth dawned on Ruel.

'Are you for Baladan?' he asked.

'Yes, Baladan – come quick and help.'

It seemed more than likely to Ruel that the child's home was in the process of being destroyed by a detachment of Oreb's soldiers – if it wasn't destroyed already. The last trace of energy drained out of him and his head drooped wearily.

'Come *on*!' the little boy wailed.

Ruel felt cold inside. He thought of all the times he'd cowered away from Oreb's savage looking bands in the last few days and he remembered the great mêlée he'd watched at the Tournament last year, imagining himself alone in the midst of it. He wouldn't have stood a chance – and that had only been for sport. In this boy's village, there would be scores of Oreb's murderous thugs killing people for real.

'I can't,' Ruel said.

'You've *got* to!' the boy shouted.

'Why?'

The boy pointed at the sword again.

'Knight,' he said. 'Have to come.'

'I'm *not* a knight,' Ruel told him, desperately.

The boy kept on pointing at the sword.

'*Knight!*' he repeated, doggedly.

'This isn't mine,' Ruel shouted at him. 'I found it somewhere. I'm not a knight.'

'*Knight!* Come quick!' the boy insisted.

'I am *not* a knight!' Ruel bellowed, and he charged at the boy, swinging his arms and roaring.

The child screamed and bolted into the trees.

Ruel stood for a moment, panting – then he wandered round and round the clearing in circles until at last he came to a halt beside the pool. Hesed had stopped drinking some time ago and the surface was now as smooth as glass. Ruel gazed at it for a while then he unslung the great sword and with a sudden awkward jerk, flung it away from him. It hit the water with a hollow splosh and sank. An instant later, Ruel dropped to his knees and plunged his arm into the pool after it, somehow thinking that the water couldn't be too deep, that he could get the sword back; but although he reached his arm into the water as far as the shoulder, his fingers didn't touch the bottom. Then he stared hard into the depths and to his astonishment, he saw the sword through the ripples he'd made. It was still sinking. It looked no bigger than a knife now but it was clearly visible, the hilt glimmering in the darkness, turning slowly as it sank. And it kept on going. Soon it looked no bigger than a pin and still it was falling away. It was a long time before it finally disappeared. When it had, Ruel buried his head in his hands and sobbed. A while later, he wandered away into the trees, not caring where he went, not caring whether he ran into Oreb's patrols, not caring whether he lived or died. Hesed remained behind, abandoned in the clearing.

After an hour tied to the stake, Nara's mouth and throat were parched – a combination of fear, nausea and real thirst. Her legs and back were aching terribly from having been bound in a standing position so long and her arms, held behind the stake by the ropes, were painful, too. Once she'd tried just relaxing and slumping – hanging from the post – but straight away, a dozen sharp pains from wrenched and twisted joints had made her gasp and struggle back upright. And all the time, her wrists and ankles were on fire from the tight ropes biting into them. Before two hours had passed, she had gone into a trance – hunger, thirst and agony had carried her away into a blurred world where everything seemed to be pulsing with pain. She was hardly conscious of anything outside herself so it took some time for her mind to register the fact that there was a pulsation going on that wasn't coming from inside her body. Slowly she struggled to make sense of it. It seemed to be something in the air – the air was throbbing. She could feel it on her face – air pushing against her cheeks in gusts. And there was a sound – a deep, menacing 'Whump! Whump! Whump!' growing louder and louder. Then suddenly a dark shadow swept over the whole clearing, like a cloud passing over the sun.

The air went icy and a shiver shook Nara's body. It seemed to awaken her and she looked up. What she saw made her mouth gape but her throat was seized up and the only sound that came out was a rasping croak. High above her, blocking the sunlight, was a shape like a flying swan but a hundred times bigger. It was just a black silhouette but she didn't need to see the details to know what it was. The Great Dragon had arrived. When it was over the clearing that was its home, it stopped beating its wings and glided in a circle then folded its wings and dived. As it plummeted, it shot out a stream of fire that hit the earth a hundred metres in front of Nara and bounced back up in a wall of flame. Immediately, the monster pulled up its long neck and beat its wings down hard to brake, sending a wave of smoke and hot air surging out across the clearing. It seemed to squash Nara back against the stake. She coughed and spluttered and her eyes were blinded for a moment – then they cleared and she saw the full horror of what was before her.

The body of the Great Dragon was like a huge mound covered in scales – each of them bigger than a giant's battle shield and all weathered by age and covered in lichen – dull yellows and rusty oranges, drab greys and greens. It would have looked for all the world like a vast, ancient rock but for the wings still stretched out high above it and the snaking neck, thick as the oldest tree in the forest. The creature took its time settling its wings against its body then craned its neck towards Nara. The head came within fifty metres of her – big and square as a house – and its brilliant golden eyes fixed themselves on her. They seemed to glow more brightly at the sight of a victim and a rumbling in its throat made a trickle of fire and smoke spill from its mouth. A huge forked tongue flicked out and round its thick, leathery lips. The stench made Nara dizzy.

But then something happened. The monster's oval pupils shrank a fraction, and the golden glow seemed to fade a little in its eyes. The neck that had been stretched out towards Nara slowly pulled back and reared up, so that the massive head was looking down at the clearing from the height of a tower. Then, to her astonishment, Nara heard a man's voice just behind her.

'Hava-nara,' it said.

Her astonishment was doubled by the fact that not just her name but her *full* name had been used – the name her father and mother used to call her, it seemed like years ago now.

The voice wasn't her father's – how could it be? He was dead and gone. But it was deep and comforting and it seemed to send a flood of energy through her exhausted body.

'Hava-nara – can you hear me?' the man said.

She struggled to make her muscles work and slowly nodded her head.

'Speak to me,' the man insisted. 'I need to know you're listening.'

She worked her mouth to try and moisten it, and at last a rough whisper came out.

'I'm listening,' she said.

'Someone will come to release you,' the man told her. 'You must take him to Helez. Tell him it's an order – from me. Do you understand?'

'Yes,' she croaked, 'I understand. But who are you?'

The man didn't reply. She felt his hand on her shoulder, squeezing gently, and another flow of power. Then he walked past her, and she saw him for the first time. He was tall, very tall, but wiry – not bulging with muscle. He had long, dark, straggly hair and was dressed in an old, cracked leather jerkin. She never saw his face – without looking back, he strode straight towards the Great Dragon. He was completely unarmed.

The afternoon was drawing to a close when Ruel saw light amongst the trees up ahead. He'd thought he was past caring about getting out of the forest so he was surprised to find himself quickening his pace. He was almost running when he finally came out into clear daylight. He was even more surprised by the disappointment he felt when he scanned the horizon and saw more trees – a great arc of trees circling round on either side to join the tree line he'd just left. He wasn't out of the forest at all. He was on the edge of another clearing – a huge one this time, but still just a clearing.

Nevertheless, the flood of light was dazzling after so long in the forest gloom and perhaps that was why it took a moment for Ruel's eyes to focus on what was in the middle of the space. But when they did, he froze. For a couple of seconds, he even stopped breathing. Right in the centre was the gigantic bulk of the Great Dragon. It was crouching on its massive haunches as if making ready to launch itself into an attack; thin trails of sulphurous smoke were curling up from its nostrils and its golden eyes – big as cartwheels – were firmly fixed on Ruel.

But nothing happened. The Dragon and Ruel remained staring at each other and the only thing that moved was the smoke of the monster's breath. Then Ruel realised that he wasn't the only person in the clearing. Perhaps twenty metres to his left, seeming as frozen as himself, stood another figure. He hardly dared shift his stare from the Dragon but turning his head slightly, he saw out of the corner of his eye that the other person was a young woman – a teenager – dressed in what appeared to be the ragged remains of a soldier's clothes. She looked dishevelled and terrified. Everything in him told him to run but after a moment, Ruel found himself edging towards her, keeping his eyes fixed on the Great Dragon every step of the way. The monster followed him with its stare but made no other movement.

As he came closer, Ruel realised the girl wasn't frozen with terror: she was tied up – tied to a stake. Still watching the Dragon, he felt for the knife that he always kept stuck in his belt.

'Quick,' she hissed, as Ruel began to cut through the rope that held her.

The knife was sharp and the girl was free in a moment but she was so cramped and weakened that when she tried to move, she almost fell. Ruel caught her then grabbed her hand and pulled her, staggering, towards the trees. He knew that the Dragon would be able to push aside the largest trunks in the forest, but at least its progress would be slowed down. Weaving in and out, the two of them might just be able to outpace it.

But as they stumbled deeper into the forest, no crashing of splintered timber came from behind them, no roar of anger – nothing. They stopped and as the frantic beating of their hearts began to slow down, they realised they were still gripping hands. They quickly released each other and waited for a while, breathing more steadily and glancing from time to time towards the clearing. Then, moved by the same instinct of curiosity, they began to creep slowly back to the fringe of the trees. They were ready to run again at any moment but there was no sign of an attack, and eventually they reached the cover of the last few trunks. The Great Dragon remained where they had last seen it, its head turned towards the place where they had entered the forest. It still hadn't made its move.

'What's your name?' Ruel asked, as they crouched in the shelter of the undergrowth, watching the Great Dragon.

She wondered for a moment which name she would use. But Hava-nara was only for special people to know – only the closest. She had never expected to hear or use it again.

'Nara,' she whispered, not taking her eyes off the huge monster in the clearing. 'Are you the person he sent?'

'The person *who* sent?'

'He said there'd be someone to release me.'

She told him about the mysterious man and Ruel knew at once that it could only have been Baladan.

'Where is he?' he said urgently. 'What happened to him?'

And his voice was so loud that the Dragon must surely have heard. But there was such anxiety in it that she didn't even think to protest. She could recognise the sound of love in a voice – she remembered it in her own when she'd cried out to know what had become of her father after he'd failed to return from the first defence of Mesaloth.

'He's gone,' she said gently. 'The Dragon ate him.'

She closed her eyes tightly as if she couldn't bear to think about it any more. But Ruel needed to know.

'Tell me what happened,' he said.

She looked at him properly now, for the first time. His eyes were fixed on hers – urgent and desperate.

'He walked straight up to it,' she told him, 'and he stood underneath its head as if he was offering himself to it – like a sacrifice. He stood there with his head bowed and it just looked at him for a while as if it didn't know what to make of him. Then it seemed to make up its mind and made a lunge for him. He didn't try to dodge or anything. He just let it snap him up. No one had come to untie me so I was sure I was going to be next but then something really strange happened. Instead of coming for me, the Dragon swayed as if it had gone dizzy and slumped back on its haunches. It must have stayed like that for ten minutes, trailing smoke and staring at me. Then you turned up.'

Before Ruel could ask her anything more, they heard a deep rumbling groan that made the earth vibrate. Their eyes jerked back to the clearing and they saw that the monster had pitched forwards so that its head was resting on the ground. It was panting – its great sides moving rapidly – and its golden eyes almost seemed to have a pleading expression in them.

'It looks ill,' Nara said, 'like it's been poisoned.'

Moments passed then the Great Dragon stirred itself as if trying to lift its head but the effort was too much for it. It gave a wretched moan and crumpled to the earth. They watched the light slowly die out of its eyes then a last trail of foul smoke parted company with its nostrils and drifted away to dissolve in the early evening air.

A gentle breeze stirred in the clearing and as Ruel and Nara stared at the body of the Great Dragon, they noticed a change come over its scales. They started to grow pale and curl up, like flakes of ash on a smouldering branch. Then one of them lifted and was carried off – and another – and another. The Dragon was blowing away. Suddenly Ruel was on his feet and running towards it. By the time he reached the body, its ribs were already showing like the frame of a roof destroyed by fire. In a desperate attempt to find what was left of his friend, Ruel started kicking wildly at the huge corpse, towering above him. If Baladan had only just been eaten, surely there must be something left of him – something that could be recovered from the monster and given a decent burial. Maybe he might even be alive. Ruel kicked his way into the body and as he did so it simply crumbled away, bones and all. The breeze grew stronger and whirled great clouds of dust high into the air like plumes of smoke. Ruel worked in a frenzy, coughing and spluttering, sometimes almost getting buried as the carcass collapsed around him, until at last there was nothing left of the monster but a massive pile of fine grey powder, rapidly being carried away by the wind. The Great Dragon had proved to be completely empty. Of Baladan there was not the slightest sign.

'Your task is completed. You've done it well.' That's what Baladan had said to him and now the words were stuck in Zethar's mind like a song he couldn't stop singing to himself. But it wasn't a happy song. Zethar was sitting by the banks of the river that flowed past Mesaloth. He was east of the city – well on the way to the sea – throwing stones into the fast running water and remembering his last minutes with Baladan. The parting had taken place at the forest fringe, no more than an hour before Ruel had caught up with their leader. Zethar had just described to Baladan, as best he could, the position of the Great Dragon's lair on the far side of the forest.

'Thank you,' Baladan had said, and had shaken his hand.

As he recalled the moment now, it seemed to Zethar that he could still feel that firm, warm grip – the rough, calloused palms.

'You are released,' Baladan went on.

There was a moment's pause and Zethar searched Baladan's face.

'Do you know everything?' he asked, at last.

'You must go now,' Baladan told him. 'One thing I *don't* know is what you will do next. Think hard. And always remember that what you have done was necessary.'

So Zethar had gone, but not where he'd planned to go – not to the ford across the river then north to the Heights of Ataroth and Abaddon, but east towards the sea.

Words of praise, thanks, and assurance – as he sat by the river throwing stones, they revolved in his mind but they gave him no pleasure and no peace. Neither did the knowledge that he had finally carried out Abaddon's orders – had taken Baladan to his death and so cleared the way for the robber chief. But cleared the way for him to do what? That was the question that tormented him. In the week since he and Baladan had parted company, Zethar had been plagued again by his waking nightmare – the memory of the Great Dragon's gaping mouth, that huge cavern of black annihilation, had racked him every time he closed his eyes.

Returning to the outskirts of the forest where he had encountered the monster the previous year had forced Zethar to admit what he had always known deep down: Abaddon, even with all the armies of the world behind him was no match for it. Baladan was right. Nothing and no one could fight the beast.

'Think hard,' that's what Baladan had said. For a week Zethar had been thinking so hard it felt as if his head would burst. Abaddon valued the kind of recklessness that Zethar specialised in and Zethar had got rid of the one stumbling block to Abaddon's rule. He could expect a generous reward from the robber – maybe a command in his army. But what was the point? Perhaps he should find his old friends, join them in Jalam's resistance to Abaddon. If there was no hope of getting rid of the Great Dragon, he could at least help rid the Old Kingdom of the upstart thief. In his heart, that was what Zethar longed to do. But the thought of what he had done to Baladan weighed him down. It felt like a rock tied to the feet of a prisoner cast into the deep. He felt it dragging him down, down – far away from air and light and the company of his friends.

Once before, Zethar had walked to the end of the Kingdom and gazed out to sea, watching birds escaping the land, flying away into the blue distance, to who-knew-what other land. He couldn't fly, but there were boats – ships – seagoing ships that could take people to the ends of the earth. Zethar threw a heavy stone as far as he could across the wide, racing river. He felt the muscles in his arm pull with the ferocity of the effort. Then he got to his feet and started to walk: east – east till the land ran out.

CHAPTER TEN

Nara led Ruel away from what was left of the Great
Dragon. But he didn't notice her doing it. He
couldn't think of anything apart from the loss of
Baladan. It was only when they were back among
the trees that he realised what was going on. She had him
by the hand, as a mother might have a child, and he
suddenly pulled away from her.

'What are you doing?' he said, roughly.

'You've got to come with me,' she told him.

'Who says?'

'The man – the one the Dragon ate.'

'Baladan – his name's Baladan,' Ruel snapped.

'It's an order,' she went on.

Nara didn't take orders. The only people she'd ever
obeyed had been her parents, and even *they* had had to be
careful how they put things to her. But somehow there
seemed no possibility that she wouldn't do what this strange
man – this Baladan – had told her.

'He said I had to take you to Helez – the village where I
got caught,' she explained.

· But then Nara hesitated.

'There might not be any village *left*, though,' she told
him, and she explained how she'd run into Oreb's patrol
on its way to destroy Helez earlier in the day.

In his mind's eye, Ruel saw the urgent face of a little boy
– saw himself chasing the child away, a deep pool, the
sword sinking.

'We'd better go and see, anyway,' Nara said, turning to
leave, but Ruel stayed where he was.

'I can't,' he muttered.

'But it's an order – from Baladan.'

He looked at her, misery in his eyes.

'I haven't got anything to fight with,' he told her.

They stared at each other for a moment then they heard a noise from the clearing behind them. It was the snort of a horse but to Ruel, it was like the sound of a familiar voice. He turned and there was Hesed, walking slowly towards them. And Baladan's mount was not alone. Behind him came Ruel's own horse, the one he'd abandoned in the forest days ago. But this wasn't the most astonishing thing – something was hanging from Hesed's saddle that sent Ruel racing towards the great horse. Sure enough, firmly secured in its scabbard was the sword that Ruel had thrown into the pool. Twined round its golden hilt was a trail of waterweed. It was impossible but Ruel was too overjoyed to waste time on questions – he tore off the weed and threw it away from him violently. 'Can you ride?' he called out to Nara, launching himself onto Hesed's back.

'Can I!' she shouted back, remembering all the hours she'd spent with her father's horses. 'Just watch!'

She sensed the burst of energy in Ruel and, willing her aching body back to life, she ran forwards and vaulted onto the other horse with an ease that astounded him. The sword, the horses – and Nara: all of them were amazing and suddenly anything seemed possible.

'Lead on then,' he said.

But in the end, it wasn't Nara who led. They hadn't been amongst the trees for long before Hesed began to pull at the reins and Ruel knew they should let the horse show the way. Nara estimated it must have taken about three hours to get from the village to the clearing but once given his head,

Hesed got them out of the forest in one. Then half an hour's cantering westwards across open downs brought them to a little rise overlooking Helez. They were expecting to find nothing but burnt-out ruins and dead bodies below but as they rode to the top of the rise, they heard the faint sound of shouting. And when they brought their horses to a halt and looked down on the village in the fading light of early evening, what they saw astonished them. Far from having been overwhelmed, the villagers were still fighting.

Although Helez had no wall round it, the outer cottages were arranged in a circle, and Ruel and Nara could see that the defenders had barricaded the small spaces between them and blocked the four narrow tracks that led into the village. It was difficult to see clearly in the twilight but it seemed to Nara that there was a surprisingly large number of people inside this rough defence work. And she couldn't quite work out how the simple villagers who'd put her on trial that morning had organised themselves so effectively. The attacking force surprised Nara, too. She'd estimated about thirty in Oreb's patrol but there looked to be more like a hundred men positioned round the village. They must have had to send for reinforcements.

'Look,' said Nara. 'There's been fighting out here, too.'

She was pointing to the sloping ground between them and the village. There were a dozen bodies scattered across it and Nara began to piece together a picture of how things must have gone: the warning brought back by her guard, Nabal; the villagers coming out to meet Oreb's patrol; a fight all the way back to the cottages; Oreb's men backing off and sending for reinforcements whilst the defenders barricaded themselves in. But something just didn't add up. She couldn't see the villagers withstanding the first attack, let alone surviving as long as this.

'Now they've had it,' Ruel said.

'Why?'

'More reinforcements.'

He nodded towards the tree line on their right and Nara saw a group of men emerge from the deepening shadows. But it wasn't a large detachment – just half a dozen strong. Maybe it was a hunting party. They certainly had something with them – but it was still alive. Then Ruel and Nara saw what it was. Two of the men were carrying a struggling child. Another pair had a second child in their grip. Suddenly the first child broke free of one of the soldiers. The man cursed.

'I've had enough of this,' he shouted and made a sudden movement.

'Stop!' one of the others barked. 'We're going to use them as hostages!'

'Forget it!' the first man said, and there was a dull silver flash in the air. He'd raised his sword over the child.

At the same moment there was the swish of a blade being drawn up on the rise.

'No!' Ruel bellowed, and charged.

The soldiers stood frozen for a moment, trying to pick out their mystery attacker in the gloom. But when Ruel was still twenty metres away they recovered, and the man with the sword swung his weapon back to finish the job. Ruel wasn't going to get there in time – but the blow never landed. There was a soft whistle to Ruel's left and the man crashed to the ground. A moment later the man still holding the child fell then one of the men holding the other tiny prisoner.

By the time Ruel reached the children, the other three men had made a run for it. Ruel brought Hesed to a halt and stared at the three bodies on the ground. Each had an arrow shaft sticking out of its chest. A moment later, Nara rode up, with reins in one hand, bow in the other and a quiver of arrows across her shoulder.

'Where did you learn to do *that*?' Ruel asked, amazed.

'You learn a lot of things in the forest,' Nara told him. 'It's a good job some of those dead men back there were archers.'

Just then there was a shriek from one of the children they'd rescued.

'Nara!'

It was a girl's voice. Nara squinted into the gloom, then jumped from her horse.

'Penina!' she replied, then staggered as her young friend crashed into her and hugged her tight.

Ruel dismounted to see to the other child and when he came close, he found he was recognised, too.

'Knight!' the little boy said. 'You came!'

'I found him wandering around in the forest,' Penina told Nara. 'He must have run off when the attack started. Remember him?'

Nara looked closer at the boy who was now clinging to Ruel's hand. During their ride to the village, she'd had time to explain to Ruel about how she'd ended up tied to the stake in the Great Dragon's clearing.

'This is the brat that got us caught,' she told him.

'He ran away from me – straight into that bunch,' Penina went on, pointing at the dead men.

But Ruel wasn't really listening. 'Reinforcements,' he muttered.

'What?' Nara asked.

'We thought this lot were reinforcements. I bet they thought *we* were reinforcements. Reinforcements might do the trick,' he explained. 'I can't shoot anything like as well as you but I bet if I got a bow, too, we could do a lot of damage to one of their positions before they even knew what had hit them. You can hardly see a thing now – they'd probably think they were being attacked by a whole detachment.'

'And if we could draw a section of their force away, maybe the villagers could break out,' Nara suggested.

'That's right,' Ruel said. 'We've got horses but I don't think *they* have – once we'd drawn them off, we could get away before they could catch us. We could even ride round and hit one of their other positions.'

Penina and the boy hid amongst the trees then Ruel and Nara collected another bow and as many arrows as they could from the corpses on the slope and picked their target. They chose a group of about thirty men positioned by the southern entrance to Helez. They were well protected in front by a wickerwork barrier but from the rear, the position was completely open. By the time the soldiers realised they were under attack and turned to charge, Nara had hit six men and Ruel two.

'Now ride,' Nara ordered, and they were away into the darkness.

Immediately they knew they were clear, they wheeled to the east ready to look for another target. But they never got to repeat their attack. They were suddenly pulled up by the sound of yelling and shouting from somewhere over to the west. They strained their eyes to see what was happening and could just make out something that looked like an assault being made on the rear of Oreb's men on the far side of Helez. Then what they'd hoped for took place – over the barricades poured the defenders of the village on the counter-attack. Ruel threw down his bow, passed his arrows to Nara and drew the Great Sword.

'For Baladan!' he roared, and charged.

Nara hesitated. Penina and the safety of the forest lay close at hand and she *had* carried out her orders – she'd brought Ruel to Helez. But a moment later, she found herself kicking her heels into her horse's sides and galloping off after Ruel.

'For Baladan,' she said quite loudly, feeling rather self-conscious and surprised at herself.

It was finished in twenty minutes. In the confusion, Oreb's men thought they were being attacked by two battalions, not to mention the forces breaking out of the village, and as darkness finally fell, what was left of them melted into the night. When the victors gathered in Helez to celebrate, it turned out that Nara's suspicions were correct: as well as the villagers, about fifty warriors crowded round the lighted bonfire in the centre of the village. None of them had much kit beyond the basics, but they looked tough and determined – none more so than their leader, who was carried shoulder high around the fire.

'Jalam!' Ruel shouted, barging through the crowd to get to his friend.

At once, Jalam jumped to the ground. Ruel had grown so much that they were the same height now and they smiled into each other's battle-weary faces, too tired to speak. Then Jalam saw the hilt of the Great Sword strapped over Ruel's shoulder.

'Where's Baladan?' he asked, confused.

Ruel looked at the ground, wondering what words he could find to explain but then he heard a voice that made his heart leap.

'I'm here.'

Ruel raised his eyes and saw, silhouetted against the fire the tall, wiry figure he knew so well.

'I've come to give you your orders,' Baladan went on. 'Step forward, the twelve.'

A space had cleared in front of Baladan and in a daze, Ruel walked into it. Then there was some pushing and jostling, and out of the crowd emerged Chilion, Rizpa, Lexa, Zilla, Zabad, and Thassi with his four friends. Ruel stared at them in amazement.

'Time enough for explanations,' Baladan went on. 'For now, all you need know, Ruel, is that the force that attacked from the west was just ten strong.' He pointed to Ruel's friends. 'They kept on searching for Jalam after you left them, and they finally found him here, doing what I sent him to do.'

'You said twelve,' Chilion interrupted. 'There's only eleven of us – where's Zethar?'

With the fire behind him, it was impossible to make out Baladan's expression but there was a pause and his voice sounded sad when he replied.

'Zethar is gone,' he said. 'I'm sorry. You have another member now to make up the twelve – her name is Nara.'

It was then that Ruel realised he hadn't seen his new friend since his charge.

'Where is she then?' Thassi asked.

There was more jostling and Nara stumbled into the light of the fire, followed by Penina and the little boy. She went up to Ruel at once.

'I had to go back for these two,' she explained.

There were angry murmurs as some of the villagers recognised Nara but Baladan cut them short.

'She has faced her punishment,' he told them, 'and she has more than repaid her debt in fighting for the boy and for you all tonight.'

They were silenced and Baladan continued with his orders to the twelve. 'Zilla, Zabad and Chilion – you are to take ten of Jalam's men and head south to Earl Jamin. Rizpa and Lexa, take ten more and go west to Earl Rakath. Thassi, take your friends and visit Earl Melech – see if he can be persuaded to join us. Ruel and Nara, take ten men and go to Kiriath. You'll find Sir Achbor and all the forest people there. Jalam, take the rest of your men and gather every loyal war band you can find. The time has come, my friends. *Now* you may use your weapons. Proclaim the news wherever you go – Baladan has destroyed the Great Dragon! Let all who would fight for the King of Kings gather on the plain at Migdal one month from today and the Heights of Ataroth shall be reclaimed!'

His voice had risen in triumph but when he finished, there was no cheering – just a deep silence. Everyone felt that something astonishing was happening – but only two people present knew just *how* astonishing. Nara had been staring hard at the dark silhouette in front of the fire. She'd only ever seen his back and had heard him speak just a handful of words but she knew well enough who he was. It was her voice that broke the silence.

'You were dead!' she said. 'The Dragon ate you!'

There were gasps and the crowd actually shrank away from Baladan as if he was a phantom. Even the friends seemed to take a step back – all except Ruel and Nara. Nara stood her ground and kept on staring but Ruel moved slowly forward. He held out his arms like a sleepwalker as if he wanted to take hold of Baladan – but Baladan held up his hand and Ruel stopped. Ruel looked into his friend's face and now he could see those deep, powerful eyes.

'I'm sorry,' Ruel whispered.

Baladan smiled.

'Tonight,' he said, softly, 'you used the sword *well*.'

A great sheet of flame blazed up from the bonfire and Ruel shielded his face. When he looked again, Baladan was gone.

Ruel couldn't sleep. He felt as if he'd been lying awake in his tent in the dark for hours. But now he could see a faint light in the sky through its open flap so he got up and slipped out into the chilly air of dawn. The month had passed, the twelve had gone on their missions and returned and the 'King's Army', as they were calling themselves, was gathered by Migdal. In the grey light, Ruel could see their tents stretching in row after row across the plain. Earls Rakath and Jamin were there with their forces – so were Sir Achbor and Jalam. But there was no sign of Earl Melech – Thassi had come back from Melech's castle with news that the Earl had given up war and would support neither side in the coming battle. Even without him though, the forces on the plain looked impressive. But Ruel was far from confident. Abaddon still had Earl Zafon and his troops, together with the Grand Army he commanded as Champion – and General Oreb's hordes had now rejoined the robber chief, pulled back from their southern campaign for this final showdown. Abaddon had a massive force and not only that, he had the best position – he had had plenty of time to prepare and had chosen to make his stand behind the earth ramparts, on the commanding Heights of Ataroth.

Ruel wandered among the tents, looking up from time to time at the dark mass of the ancient mound. Today, on its slopes, everything would be decided. It seemed strange to Ruel that the future of a whole Kingdom, perhaps for generations to come, could be decided in just a few hours but that was surely what would have happened here before the sun set again. One or two others started to emerge from their tents as the light strengthened and Ruel saw a small campfire flicker into life between the rows. He drifted towards it and when he came near, he saw that a solitary figure was squatting there, holding something out on a stick to the flames. The man's long dark hair masked his face but Ruel would have recognised his cracked leather jacket anywhere.

Baladan looked up as Ruel approached and offered him the strip of meat he'd been cooking. But Ruel waved it away. His stomach was churning and he couldn't bring himself to eat. He was anxious about the coming battle but it was more than that – the sudden sight of his friend was too disturbing for Ruel simply to share food with him as if this was an ordinary meeting. He stood over Baladan with a look of anger in his face.

'What happened?' he demanded. 'You were dead – then you were alive again – then you disappeared. I haven't known what to think this last month. Or what to say to people. I thought you must have been a *ghost. Are* you a ghost?'

Baladan took a bite of the meat and chewed for a moment.

'Is Jalam a ghost?' he asked. 'Do ghosts eat breakfast?'

'It's not possible,' Ruel declared.

Baladan motioned for him to sit and the two stared at each other for a moment then Ruel reluctantly joined him by the crackling fire.

'There are more things possible than you can understand,' Baladan told him, at last. 'There are powers that are stronger than Abaddon, stronger than dragons – even the Great Dragon – powers that are stronger even than death.'

Ruel spent a moment taking this in – trying to fit it into the picture of all that had happened.

'You *knew* you'd come back to life again?' he asked.

Baladan nodded.

'But if you *knew*, why were you so... Why were you *shaking* that night on the Heights? Were you afraid? Why, if you knew?'

'*Knowing* is one thing,' Baladan replied, quietly. '*Doing* is something else entirely – even for me.'

He lifted the side of his jacket to show some of the many pale scars that marked his body.

'You've seen these often enough,' he said. 'Do you think these wounds didn't hurt? Do you think I feel pain any less than you – or fear it any less?'

There was a long silence as Baladan finished his breakfast and when he spoke again, he was brisk and very business-like.

'I have orders to give,' he said.

'For the battle?' Ruel asked.

'For *after* the battle,' Baladan told him. 'And you are to announce them. They'll want to crown a king – maybe Achbor, maybe Jalam, maybe even you!'

'But won't *you* be King?' Ruel asked.

'Tell them there are to be no more kings on the throne here,' Baladan replied. 'I didn't come to start a new line of kings but to remind the people of their allegiance to the King of all Kings. There won't be a single ruler to establish the King's justice but you and the rest of the twelve are to form a Grand Council to govern the land as the King would like. The last of the dragons need clearing and there will always be people like Abaddon to deal with – so the Great Earls, including Zafon if he's willing, are to provide forces to do the job. Jalam will command them in the north and Achbor in the south. You must send Oreb north of the border as your emissary to the Northern Realm – his mission is to agree an alliance. That should keep him out of mischief – offer to reward him well but don't pay up until you *see* results! Oh, and the history of all that has happened must be recorded. Lord Zemira must write a song – it's to be called "The Song of the *New* Kingdom" – from this time on, the Kingdom is "old" no longer. It has been reborn.'

Ruel felt dazed. 'Won't *you* give the orders,' he said, when Baladan had finished. 'How is anyone going to take any notice of me?'

'They'll have to,' Baladan told him. '*You're* going to be Leader of the Council.'

Then he got up and wiped his fingers on his long thighs.

'But what if I get killed?' Ruel said. 'What if Jalam does, or Achbor? What if we don't win?'

Baladan didn't reply.

'You *are* going to lead us, aren't you?'

There was another pause.

'I've fought my battle,' Baladan said. 'Now you must fight yours.'

Disappointment and foreboding seemed to weigh Ruel down to the ground.

'When will I see you again?' he said, quietly.

Baladan stooped, took him by the shoulders, gently raised him to his feet and held his eyes.

'Ruel, you'll never see me again – not in *this* Kingdom,' he said. 'But if you look in your heart, you'll know that I'm always with you there.'

The mixture of power and love in Baladan's gaze and the confusion and misery in Ruel's mind made the young man's chin sink on his chest and he stared at the ground.

'And when you finally come to my castle,' Baladan went on, gently, 'we'll be together *there* for ever – I promise.'

Mention of the castle made Ruel close his eyes and when he did, he found that he saw it all again – as vividly as if he was at the edge of the mysterious, radiant valley once more: the golden corn, the sparkling river, the crystal walls and fluttering pennants of the castle of the King. At once, his sadness and anxiety blew away like the dust of the Dragon and his heart was suddenly filled with an emotion too wonderful to describe. 'My castle'… '*My* castle!' At last, with a flash of unshakeable certainty, he felt that he knew the true identity of the friend who had travelled with him all this time. This was the third year of his quest to find the King and now he finally realised that he'd succeeded on the very day he'd set out. He opened his eyes and took one quick look at the face of Baladan, smiling warmly at him, then sank to his knees before his friend and bowed his head again.

'My Lord,' he said, in a shaking voice.

A moment later Ruel heard the drawing of a sword and felt the weight of its blade rest first on one shoulder then on the other.

He heard Baladan's voice, speaking over him: 'Rise, Sir Ruel of the Forest – Leader of my Council.'

Then nothing. Ruel was too happy to move and it was only when he heard another familiar voice that he opened his eyes and looked up. It was Nara.

'Come on,' she said. 'He told you to rise – there's work to do.'

She was half armed for battle and was just sheathing a short sword that had been issued to her.

'I came looking for you,' she explained. 'He asked for my sword.'

'Where is he?' Ruel asked.

'He walked off amongst the tents,' she said. 'He's just – '

But when she pointed in the direction Baladan had taken, he was nowhere to be seen.

~~~

The sun was fully up and it seemed to shine on a field of scattered treasure. White light winked and flashed from the helmets of soldiers drawn up in their thousands on the plain of Migdal and everywhere among them were the rich colours of their plumes and banners. On the right wing were the banners of Earl Jamin – a golden sun on a white background bordered with gold. All the helmets of his knights and commanders were decorated with yellow and orange feathers, like flickers of flame. The left wing was made up of Earl Rakath's forces. Their banners were in red and green quarters, and red and green feathers bobbed on the top of their helmets. The centre was commanded by Sir Achbor, with Jalam as his lieutenant, and it was made up of every band of warriors in the Kingdom that was loyal to the cause of Baladan and the King of Kings.

It was in the centre that Ruel and Nara had taken up their positions, side by side, with the younger members of the twelve. They formed part of the cavalry, under Jalam's command. In front of them were ranks of archers. And in front of the archers were the infantry lines, Achbor at their head. If it came to an assault on the Heights, the infantry would have to climb and fight their way over the ramparts and up the slope. But if Abaddon could be drawn out onto the plain, then the cavalry would ride to meet him. But for an hour after the King's Army had mustered in battle order, nothing happened. They could see the solid wall of Abaddon's troops lining the ramparts at the base of the Heights and the dense mass of reserves drawn up on the summit but it didn't seem as if he intended to make a move.

'Why should he?' Nara said to Ruel, as they discussed the situation. 'I wouldn't if I was him. He can sit there as long as he likes and let us wear ourselves out attacking him.'

'We could just camp here and starve him out,' Ruel suggested.

Nara knew all about sieges and she was about to make some comment on how long that could last when suddenly there *was* some movement from Abaddon's position. The whole line of troops guarding the outer rampart climbed over the defences and came charging across the plain. But it was a strange, ragged charge, with no shouting and blaring of trumpets. And from what Ruel and Nara could see it seemed to have left confusion behind.

'Look,' Ruel said. 'That's Abaddon.'

There was no mistaking the giant figure. He was standing up on the top of the second rampart and waving his arms furiously, yelling after the charging soldiers. Then he started issuing commands to the troops on the inner defences.

'That doesn't look as if things are going to plan,' Nara commented, as soldiers started scrambling over the second rampart and hurriedly taking up the positions the charging mob had just vacated.

Ruel swallowed hard as the advancing force drew near. 'This'll be our job,' he said. There was a tremor in his voice and his hands were shaking – he wished Baladan were there. Then he remembered what his friend had said – 'if you look in your heart...' He closed his eyes for a moment and pictured Baladan's face, full of power and warmth, then opened them again and unsheathed the sword. Since it had been passed to Ruel, it no longer exploded with light when it left its scabbard as it used to do when Baladan owned it, but it was still a mighty weapon – and the hands that held it now were steady.

All along the cavalry line, weapons were made ready, fingers tightened on the horses' reins, and the ranks of foot soldiers in front of them opened up to let the riders gallop through. But Jalam held steady and no order to charge was given. Soon the attackers were close enough for Ruel and Nara to see their faces and Ruel suddenly had a shock. They were being led by a huge man with a shining bald head and it was someone he knew – Halak the blacksmith from Ruel's own village.

At the moment that Ruel recognised him, Halak threw

back his head and yelled, 'For Baladan!'

His whole force took this as their signal and every one of them started shouting, 'For Baladan! For Baladan!'

Sir Achbor barked a command down the line and the infantry ranks of the King's Army simply stood in open order and let Halak's men pour through without a blow being struck. As soon as they were safely inside the King's lines, Halak's troops started cheering and shaking hands with everyone around them. And when they realised what had happened, the King's Army let out a roar of triumph – at least a third of Abaddon's troops had deserted at a stroke and joined the forces of the King.

Ruel couldn't bear the mystery. He left his position and trotted up to Jalam.

'What's going on?' he asked.

Jalam was beaming all over his face.

'We got word last night,' he said. 'A bunch of deserters slipped away from the Heights after dark to warn us about their plan. Apparently news has got round that Baladan's killed the Great Dragon and now half Abaddon's men don't want to fight for him any more – they were only sticking with him because they thought there was no other option.'

Inside the ramparts, Abaddon was fuming. The two armies had been evenly matched, but now that Halak had stripped him of his front line, the numbers had swung against him. He knew that soldiers had been slipping away for the last fortnight – ever since rumours about Baladan's victory over the Great Dragon had started to circulate. He'd told his troops that the story was a pack of lies and he'd executed any deserters he'd managed to capture, but if he was going to hold his army together, he knew that he had to score a decisive victory and quickly. And if he was going to achieve that today, he desperately needed something to give him the initiative. Then half an hour after Halak's desertion, he got it. A lookout shouted and scrambling to the top of the mound, Abaddon saw an army marching towards him from the north east. The blue and yellow banners told him it was Earl Melech, coming to save the day.

Abaddon had sent a detachment of his riders to Melech's castle a week ago, threatening to tear it to pieces stone by stone and its owner limb from limb if the Earl didn't come to join forces with him at once. So this was the response – later than it might have been but better late than never, Abaddon thought. He quickly calculated distances, speed of advance, weight of numbers, and made his decision. If the opposing army's leaders had any sense, they'd never let Melech's forces get safely inside the ramparts without attacking them so the thing to do was send Melech's troops straight into the attack themselves. Abaddon decided that if he stormed out, too, their combined forces stood a good chance of driving the enemy from the field. And anyway, Abaddon was angry – very angry – he needed to be smashing skulls. He dispatched a squad of his fastest riders to Melech with his orders and got his men ready for action.

Twenty minutes later, Earl Melech's cavalry came cantering in battle order round the eastern flank of the Heights and with perfect timing, Abaddon deployed his own horsemen. He led them himself and Earl Zafon rode at his side. As the two forces came into line, Abaddon bellowed and his troops sped forward at full gallop, with Melech's cavalry keeping pace on his left. The gigantic robber wore no armour – in his fury and eagerness for battle, he'd sent his squires flying in a clattering heap of steel plates – and he was a terrifying sight, charging his enemies with no more protection than a shield and his old studded jacket.

When Abaddon's cavalry were halfway across the open ground between them and the King's Army, there was a sound like a sudden gust of wind and a hail of arrows struck them, sending scores of horses and riders writhing to the ground. But despite his lack of armour, Abaddon was untouched and galloped on at the head of his troops, bellowing and swinging a huge mace above his head. He seemed invincible. The enemy infantry in front of him opened ranks, ready for their cavalry to make a counter charge and Abaddon roared so fiercely that many of the King's horses shied. But in the fury of his charge, the robber chief didn't see was what was happening to his left. Before the shower of arrows had even landed, Melech had veered his own troops wide so that few of them were hit and now he was leading them in a broad arc far out on the wing, not to *attack* the King's Army but to *join* it. The mass of his infantry marching on behind already had orders to bypass Abaddon's position and join up with the opposition.

It was only when Abaddon realised that his forces were being pushed back in the mêlée that followed the crashing together of the cavalry, that he suspected treachery and looked round frantically for Melech and his troops. There was not a blue and yellow plume, or shield or banner to be seen. The Earl and his cavalry were now safely drawn up behind the King's lines. Abaddon was not so crazed that he didn't realise at once he would have to withdraw but as he was about to give the order, he saw the red and green banners of Earl Rakath begin to move on the right. The Earl was clearly going to gallop across Abaddon's rear and try to cut him off from the Heights. Abaddon's only hope was his remaining force on top of the mound under Oreb's command. They would have to attack Rakath's troops and keep a way open for their leader's retreat – surely Oreb would have the sense to see that.

Up on the Heights, General Oreb could see it all *very* clearly. He knew that he could hold Rakath off long enough for Abaddon to get back to the ramparts – but what then? With Halak's deserters and Melech's forces joining the opposition, the numbers were now heavily against Abaddon. Oreb considered for a moment, then sent orders to his officers and began to lead his troops down from the Heights of Ataroth.

With relief, Abaddon saw Oreb coming to his rescue and yelled out the order to retreat. Fighting ferociously, what was left of his cavalry managed to hack their way clear of their enemies and gallop back towards the ramparts. And now it became a race – Abaddon heading back to the Heights, Jalam's cavalry tearing after him, Earl Rakath's force speeding in from the western flank – and Oreb. Oreb should have been veering west too, to block Earl Rakath's path, but to his horror, Abaddon saw that his general was heading straight towards him. Abaddon could see Oreb now at the head of his troops and he waved his arms wildly at him.

'Right!' he shouted. 'To your right, man! Take Rakath!'

And then he realised what was happening.

At the same time as Earl Rakath's force smashed into Abaddon's flank, Oreb's troops drove head on into him, stopping his retreat in its tracks; and a moment later, Jalam's cavalry crashed in from the rear. It was over in minutes. Earl Zafon and many others surrendered at once. Those who didn't were cut to pieces. It was hard to establish what finally killed the Earl of the Middle Lands, Abaddon the robber chief. It could have been the stab in the back from Oreb's short sword or the mighty swipe from Jalam's blade that took the giant's head from his body but then again, when that head hit the ground, it had an arrow buried in one great bull's eye – and Nara was a deadly shot.

The afternoon was drawing to a close. Ruel stood beside Hesed and surveyed the field of combat. He was exhausted, not just physically but deep inside. He'd come through the battle unharmed but he felt battered and bruised in his heart and mind in a way that he hadn't known was possible. He leaned against Hesed for support as he watched people picking amongst the bodies, trying to find friends and loved ones and bandage the wounds of the injured. To Ruel, there seemed to be so many bodies, and yet in the end, this had only been a small battle, he realised, with no more than a part of each army engaged. The groaning and whimpering of the injured was pitiful to hear. As he took everything in, he was more aware of feelings than thoughts. He had a dim sense of relief – relief that they'd won the day and that he had survived – but apart from that, he felt empty. There was no rejoicing in him at all.

He was relieved, too, that his friends were still alive. He could see Jalam in the distance, leading away a group of prisoners under guard. And Sir Achbor stood close by, giving instructions to a circle of infantry officers. His wife – Ruel's sister, Safir – was at his side. Naama, Ruel's mother, had also followed her husband to battle. Ruel's father, Maaz, had marched north from Kiriath with the forest people and he and Naama were now sitting with Halak and some others from Hazar – Chilion, Thassi and his four friends. They all seemed subdued and were exchanging only the occasional word. Ruel's mother and father were holding hands – something he rarely saw them do. Close to this group, Lexa was supporting her sister Rizpa who had a wounded shoulder. Zilla was smoothing a healing ointment onto the gash while Zabad prepared a bandage. In view of their age,

Zilla and Zabad had not been in the front line during the battle but had formed part of a chain supplying bundles of arrows to the archers. Now they were helping attend to the injured.

Nara was standing close to Ruel as he scanned the scene. She'd come to find him as soon as the fighting was over. The sight of so much bloodshed was nothing new to her but she could see that it was affecting Ruel deeply and it was a long time before she tried to speak to him.

'Zilla's going to need buckets of that,' she said quietly, pointing at the old woman, carefully applying her ointment.

She thought that Ruel wasn't going to reply but after a few moments, he looked at her.

'I'm glad you're here, Nara,' he murmured.

They watched Zilla and Zabad finish with Rizpa then move on to another patient, and at last Ruel seemed to wake up.

'Let's go and help,' he suggested.

They started to walk towards Zilla and Zabad but Nara took hold of Ruel's sleeve to stop him.

'Ruel,' she said, 'will you do something for me?'

'What?'

'Will you call me Hava-nara?'

'Why?' he asked.

'It's just a sort of special name, that's all. Would you – will you use it?'

Ruel looked at her, puzzled, but she was staring at the blood-spattered ground and wouldn't meet his eyes.

'Hava-nara,' he said, trying it out.

She looked up at him and smiled – then, together, they went to join Zilla and Zabad in their healing work.

author's note

I was sitting at home, relaxing one evening towards the end of the week when the phone rang. It was my old friend Michael Taylor. He was just ringing to let me know he'd be coming to hear me preach at the children's service at our church on Sunday.

'Great, see you there,' I said, and put the phone down. Then I put my head in my hands. I'd *forgotten* it was a children's service, and I'd been busily preparing a sermon for *adults* all week! I lay down on the settee, closed my eyes, and asked God to send me a story to tell on Sunday – and be quick about it! He did, and that's how the stories in the *Rumours of the King* trilogy got started.

The story I told that Sunday morning was inspired by one of the Bible readings for the day, which was from the Gospel of Mark. Afterwards, I wondered if I could write more about the dragon slayer and his friends, using the stories of Jesus as my inspiration. So that's what I did, and I soon found there was enough material to make three books!

Steve Dixon

If you've enjoyed this book, look out for the other two titles in the *Rumours of the King* Trilogy. *The story begins in…*

OUT OF THE SHADOWS

'A horrible feeling, like something squashing his heart, sent Ruel racing from the forest. He arrived just in time to see two men leading the latest sacrifice up towards the trees. Ruel saw at once what his heart had known already. The victim was Safir.'

The village of Hazar has lived under the shadow of The Reaper for a long time. People are taken and never seen again. But when Ruel's sister is chosen, he decides to find out what happens to the sacrifices; he decides to fight back.

ISBN 1 85999 671 X

The story continues in…

WHAT THE SWORD SAID

'A challenge!' Rakath boomed. 'Earl Melech is to host a Grand Tournament in the autumn of the year. Contestants are invited from every land in the Old Kingdom to find a Champion. But this will be no ordinary champion, this will be a Champion to lead a Grand Army. But what is the army *for*? Who will it fight?'

He left a dramatic pause and scanned his audience for a moment before continuing.

'Why, none other than the dragons!'

Ruel's friends have been scattered to the four winds at Baladan's orders. As each travels a difficult road they find themselves drawn to Melech's tournament. But what are they meant to do there? And does Baladan have a plan?

ISBN 1 85999 672 8

You can buy these books at your local Christian bookshop, or online at www.scriptureunion.org.uk/publishing or call Mail Order direct: 08450 706 006